Erin struggled to maintain her authority as teacher in the backwoods school.

"What is it, Enlo? I thought I made myself clear. You're to go home."

Enlo lurched into the schoolhouse. Wherever he had been, it was obvious that he had not stopped drinking. He leaned toward Erin until he was just a few inches from her face.

"Now, Teacher," he said. "It's Christmas, and I didn't even git no presents."

Erin gathered his gifts from her desk and held them up to him. "All right, here is the candy and mittens we gave to the rest of the students. Have a happy Christmas, Enlo. Now, I really think you should go on your way."

Enlo smiled. "Thank you, Teacher, but I come to git my real present. I ain't had my Christmas kiss."

The look in Enlo's eyes frightened her. Erin stepped back, trying to put her desk between them, but he grabbed her arm.

"Enlo, you'd better let go of me. Douglas will be back in here any minute."

Enlo pulled her over toward him. "Let the Preacher come," he said. "I'll show him how to treat a lady."

CHERYL TENBROOK'S numerous Christian articles, short stories, and scripts have won her many national awards. Among her honors she has been recognized at the Lamplighter's Inspirational Writers' Conference. Her work has been published in *Youth Leadership*, *Sunday Digest,* and *Straight,* as well as other Christian publications. She makes her home in Kansas.

Lost Creek Mission

Cheryl Tenbrook

Heartsong Presents

To my dad
and my husband Gayle
for always believing.
John 3:30

A note from the Author:
*I love to hear from my readers! You may write to me
at the following address:*

**Cheryl Tenbrook
Author Relations
P.O. Box 719
Uhrichsville, OH 44683**

ISBN 1-55748-693-X

LOST CREEK MISSION

Cover illustration by Brian Bowman.

PRINTED IN THE U.S.A.

one

The engine lurched, then chugged slowly away from the station, belching out cinders that tapped lightly on the roof. Finally, about a mile outside the city limits, the train began to pick up speed, and the staccato rhythm of wheels on tracks echoed Erin's excited heartbeat. She tucked her skirts in and tried to look dignified, but she couldn't help smiling.

Erin's friends at the orphanage hadn't been able to understand why she would want to become a missionary. Every girl at the Manchester Orphanage longed for the day when she could have a home of her own—and the only way to get a home was to find a husband. Why spend a year teaching in a backwoods school, they reasoned, when Erin was finally old enough to marry and have a real family? After all, Erin wasn't likely to find a husband out in the woods, was she?

But Erin believed she had heard God calling her to the Lost Creek Mission, and she had to obey. Besides, who could say? God just might find her a husband even out in the backwoods of Missouri. Her smile widened for a moment, and then she pushed the thought firmly to the back of her mind.

She leaned toward the window, watching as the landscape changed as they continued on south from St. Louis. Wide acres of carefully cleared farmland gave way to steep hills and dense stands of trees. The well-maintained roadways near the tracks fell behind, and now Erin could see only rough wagon trails that cut through pastures and disappeared into the woods. Above the train bed's banks, tall bluffs of orange-white rock jutted through the thin soil.

Shadows already covered the train station when they finally pulled into Mineral Point. Erin gathered her belongings and checked into the hotel next to the depot. She ate the supper she had packed for herself at the orphanage, then quickly prepared for bed, but she barely slept at all that night. Lying on the lumpy straw mattress, her mind spun in circles.

"I wonder what Douglas Teterbaugh will be like?" she thought. She knew that Reverend Teterbaugh had also been assigned to Lost Creek Mission and that he was a recent seminary graduate, but that was all the mission board had told her.

At daylight, Erin was back on the train. Rain spattered on the roof, and the sound of raindrops and the train's rhythmic motion lulled her back to sleep. Exhausted from her sleepless night, she slept while the train wound its way deeper into Missouri. Not until the car rocked from side to side, bumping her head against the window, did she open her eyes.

On the other side of the window she saw thick tree trunks an arm's length from the tracks. The underbrush was so dense she could see into the woods for only a few feet. Used to city life, Erin had never realized before how many shades of green there were. Amid the thick leaves, wild flowers bloomed, black-eyed Susans and Queen Anne's lace and little purple blossoms that grew close to the ground.

As the train pulled into the Potosi station, Erin repinned her hat and freshened up as best she could. She was certain that the other passengers could hear her heart pounding as she thought of meeting Reverend Teterbaugh on the platform. How many times had the headmistress at the orphanage told her, "A lady must always be calm of voice and confident in manner." Erin took a deep breath and started down the aisle.

The depot was a busy place for such a small town. People were milling about on the platform, greeting arrivals and unloading freight from the boxcars. Erin stepped down. At least the rain had stopped.

A slim, dark-haired man was standing near the station door. His eyes met Erin's and he hurried to her.

"You must be Miss Corbett," he said.

"Yes, and you're Reverend Teterbaugh."

He smiled. "I must say I'm delighted. Not all missionaries come with such a charming face."

Erin laughed. "You're very bold for a minister, sir."

"So I've been told," the Reverend admitted. "Do let me take your valise. I'll see to it that the rest of your luggage is properly handled."

"Thank you, Reverend Teterbaugh."

"Please, call me Douglas. Teterbaugh is such a long name."

"All right, Douglas, if you'll call me Erin. When did you arrive?"

"On the 5:30 from Cape Girardeau, a most ungodly time of the morning. But I suppose I'll soon have to get used to such hours."

"Yes. I imagine country people are early risers," Erin said. "Did Dr. Tichenor tell you who would meet us at the Potosi station?"

"No, his letter only said that someone from Lost Creek would be here to load our things and drive us to the Gillam farm. I would think perhaps Mr. Gillam might come himself, since we'll be staying in his home."

"I wonder what type of house it is. . .do you think it might be a log cabin?"

"Good heavens, I hope not," Douglas said. "But I suppose anything is possible."

"It's all so exciting. In a few hours we'll begin what may be the greatest adventure of our lives."

Erin ignored the amused expression that flickered across the Reverend's face. She picked up her reticule and walked to the edge of the platform.

No one was there except a grizzled old man who stood holding the reins of two mules at the far end of the station. The man caught sight of them and started walking in their direction. Erin had never seen anyone quite like him. His clothes were creased and worn. Over his work shirt he wore a vest which had, at one time, been white with red pinstripes. A straw hat, curled up at the sides, rested on the back of his egg-shaped head. He walked with his toes pointed out and his knees bent as if he were used to traveling on ground that often gave way underneath him.

"Douglas, you don't suppose that he's the one. . ."

"I am afraid so. Put on your best smile. Your adventure is about to begin."

two

When the man was a few feet in front of them, he paused to spit a thick stream of tobacco juice on the ground. Erin hoped her face did not show her revulsion. The man studied Douglas and Erin thoughtfully. He seemed in no particular hurry.

"How do," he said at last. "Would you be the folks that I was sent to fetch to the Gillam place?"

Douglas reached out his hand. "Why yes, I'm Rev. Douglas Teterbaugh, and this is Miss Erin Corbett. You must be Mr. Gillam?"

The old man laughed loudly, displaying an odd assortment of yellowed teeth. "No, my name's Jube Taylor. Pleased t'make your acquaintance."

Mr. Taylor shook Douglas' hand as if he were working a pump handle, then tipped his hat toward Erin. "Pleasure to know you too, ma'am. My, but ain't you a looksome young thing." A mosquito landed on Mr. Taylor's neck. He gave it a sharp swat, then he continued, "Tucker Gillam, he asked me would I drive out here and carry you back to his place, it bein' a busy time out on the farm. We might ought t'git your things loaded up quick, if you don't mind. We had a gully warsher of a rain this morning and like as not the cricks and branches are rised up. I'd jist as soon make the most of the ride 'fore it gits dark."

Erin looked at Douglas, and then back at Mr. Taylor. "But, it's not yet ten o'clock. Will it take that long to get to our destination?"

"Ma'am? Oh, you mean to the Gillams'. Well, we could make it a little sooner, except that I got to drop off some supplies to old man Doss at the Berryman store. But don't you fret, ole Jube'll git you there in a whip stitch. Preacher, you start haulin' your things over and I'll bring the wagon round where we can load it easier."

Mr. Taylor brought the team to the front of the station. To her dismay, Erin saw that he was driving an old farm wagon fitted with a single seat. If the rain started up again, it would be a long day indeed.

Douglas carried their things over to the edge of the platform and Mr. Taylor loaded them. "This is it," Douglas said at last. "Except for that band box and a valise."

"Great blue-nosed frog tadpoles! I ain't never seen such truck for jist two people. I sure do hope them old mules can pull all this hoo-rah." Mr. Taylor shook his head and loaded the last bag.

Erin felt guilty since most of that luggage was hers. "Mr. Taylor? I'm afraid I may have packed too many things," she said. "Perhaps we could leave some of them here and have them shipped later."

Mr. Taylor pulled the rope tight across the top of a trunk. "Name's Jube," he said gruffly. He tied off the last knot and looked up. "Aw, I reckon we can make it all right. Besides, they ain't nobody t'ship it with and heaven knows when it'd be 'fore anyone could haul it out for you."

Jube passed his hand over several days' worth of beard. "Miz Erin, you best let me heft you over to the wagon; this mud would suck in a fair-sized hog today."

"Thank you Mr. . .uh. . .Jube, but I'm sure I can manage."

"Suit yourself, then," he said. "Let's git started."

Unfortunately, Jube was right. By the time Erin had made her way to the wagon, both her shoes and the hem of her skirt were caked with mud. Once she was seated, she looked back and saw Douglas carefully picking his way around the worst puddles. Jube turned in Douglas' direction and sent a squirt of tobacco juice to the ground.

"C'mon, Preacher," he called. "Them shoes'll clean up. We got a ways to go."

Chastened, Douglas took a determined step into mud that oozed over his shoe tops. He climbed onto the wagon seat just as Jube called to the mules and sent them on their way.

Douglas kicked at the mud on his shoes as they rattled out of town. "Tell me, Jube," he said. "Does the road improve further along, or will it be this rough all the way?"

Jube laughed and spit on the side of the road. "Preacher, this road is smooth as a baby's behind compared to the bone rattler going into Lost Crick. That road ain't nothing but stumps and gullies. Some of it's so hilly you could stand up straight and lick a rock. It's that part of the trip that takes so turrible long." Jube looked over at Douglas. "You ain't never been round these parts before, have you, Preacher?"

"No, I'm afraid not. All I know is what the missionary board told me."

"Well, anything you need to know, you jist ask ole Jube. I reckon I'm acquainted with every man, woman, and coon hound from here to Steeleville."

"How many people are there in Lost Creek?" Douglas asked.

"Oh, there be ten or twelve families in hollerin' distance, and a few more spread about. Course, there's some that ain't got sense enough to pound sand in a rathole, but by and large, most folks work hard and weed their own row."

"Are there many school-aged children, Jube?" Erin asked.

"Yes, ma'am, I reckon jist about every family's got a youngun or two for your school. The womenfolk birth babies real regular 'round here."

Erin could feel her cheeks warming. Jube certainly did not mince words.

"They got the old schoolhouse fixed up real pretty," Jube continued. "Tucker even went and had it painted up white as duck down."

"This Tucker, is he related to Daniel Gillam?" Douglas asked.

"Surely, Preacher. Tucker is Daniel's oldest boy." Jube looked uncomfortable. "Ain't nobody told you that Daniel passed on?"

"Mr. Gillam is dead?"

"Well, I hope so, Preacher. We sure as the world buried him. Daniel was nailin' on new roof boards up top of the schoolhouse last spring when some old wood gave way and sent him head first smack into the ground. He lasted on a while, but he was so busted up there wasn't nothin' nobody could do for him. Daniel was a real good man, well thought of by everybody."

"I hope the people of Lost Creek will still be willing to support the mission despite Mr. Gillam's death," Erin said.

"Now, don't you fret about that, ma'am. Tucker has a younger brother, name of Ben, who'll be in your school. Tucker give his daddy a solemn deathbed promise to see to it that the school gits opened. If Tucker Gillam says it's right to have school again, like as not you'll have a whole bate of younguns the first day."

"Have they had a school here before?" Erin asked.

"Yes'm. We had a widower man who taught real regular till he passed on six or seven years ago. Since then it seems like none of the teachers that came along were very lasty like. Haven't had any school for near four years now. You'll be the first lady teacher ever in these parts."

"What about the church?" Douglas asked. "Have you ever had a full-time pastor before?"

"Land no! Closest every-Sunday church is out past Berryman. Last winter we had a circuit rider settle in. . .ole boy by name of Silas Butler. He preaches at the schoolhouse once a month, if he don't git hung up somewheres else on his route."

"The schoolhouse? Don't you have a church building?" Douglas asked.

Jube reached in his pocket for some fresh tobacco. "Speakin' frank and actual, Preacher, most folks here don't see the need t'waste wood on a church to use once a week when we got the schoolhouse."

Douglas was obviously not pleased with this news. Erin thought perhaps she should change the subject.

"Jube, what is the Gillam place like?" she asked. "Is it a nice farm?"

Jube slapped one of the mules with the reins to get it back to the center of the road. "Oh, yes'm, it's the grandest farm around," he said. "Tucker's grandaddy homesteaded some of the best bottom land on the Cortoway River. Course, that was away long back before the war, when it was real wild country. Each generation has built on till it's a glory of a place. They got a bought lumber house with one floor piled right on top of the other. High livin' ain't gone to Tucker's head, though. He's hard workin' and honest, like his daddy. Still, ain't nobody who'll cross Tucker Gillam—he's big enough to go bear huntin' with a switch."

So far, Erin had not heard Jube mention anything about a Mrs. Gillam. Surely she wasn't being sent to a bachelor's home. "Jube, what about Mr. Gillam's wife?" she asked.

"Miz Gillam died when Ben was jist a little shaver, and Tucker ain't showed much interest in a wife lately. But if you're frettin' about staying in a house full of menfolks, you can rest easy. Mattie Cotter's been keeping house for the Gillams since before Ben was borned. She ain't never had much use for me, but she'll see you won't come to no harm."

Erin's attention was drawn away from Jube's words by the sound of rushing water. They came around the bend and Erin saw a stream flowing right across the roadbed ahead of them. She imagined it was normally a shallow stream, but the rain had caused it to rise and run fast. Jube kept talking, seemingly unconcerned about what was ahead.

"Are we going to cross that?" Erin asked.

"Oh yes'm, that water ain't even axle deep. This here's Haunted Spring. It never gits up high enough to cause any trouble. Ain't you never forded a stream before?"

"No, I guess I haven't. Isn't it dangerous?"

"On bigger cricks, in high water, surely. But not with a little one like this. You jist hang on to your hat."

The wagon splashed into the water. Erin's breath caught in her throat as the wheels rolled into the stream bed, but they pulled up safely on the other side. Erin realized she was clinging to Douglas' arm and quickly folded her hands in her lap.

They stopped to eat at a place called Webb Hollow. The mules drank from a small pond and then ate grain out of the nose bags Jube buckled over their heads. After the team was fed, Jube brought out some crackers and cheese from a tow sack under the wagon seat and passed them around. They all drank from a jug of water covered with wet burlap to keep it cool. When the mules had rested, Erin followed Douglas and Jube back to the wagon, and Jube urged the animals on once again.

They had gone on just a little way when a horse and buckboard appeared up ahead. Suddenly, Jube let out a yell that would have awakened the dead.

"What's wrong?" Erin asked. "Is that man an outlaw?"

"Outlaw?" Jube laughed. "Why no, ma'am. Ain't you never heard nobody whoop howdy? Young James, you come here and show the new schoolmarm you ain't no outlaw."

The stranger pulled his rig up even with theirs, and Jube made the introductions. "James Doss, this here is Rev. Teterbaugh and Miz Corbett. James' daddy owns the store at Berryman. Why are you traipsin' about here in the shank of the day, boy? Can't your daddy keep you busy?"

"He sent me out here to find you. Asa Keller came through a while back and said Lost Crick was rising fast. Daddy thought I'd best meet you and fetch them supplies on in so you could be sure and ford it in the daylight."

"I appreciate that," Jube said. "Jump on down and we'll switch the load. Preacher, we could use another hand, if you'd oblige us."

Douglas sighed, then he stepped down and walked to the back of the wagon. When the transfer was done, Jube and Douglas climbed back on the seat, and Jube raised his hand toward James. "Thank you till you're better paid," he said.

James waved back. "Y'all take care crossin' the crick."

They had to slow down considerably as soon as they turned onto the Lost Creek road. From what Erin could see, the road was just a narrow path of stumps and ruts cut out of the wilderness. Still, she was grateful that they were finally close to their destination.

Jube looked over at Erin. "Beauty of a road, ain't it? Gits wamperjawed like this every time we git a good rain. The water ruts up the road so bad it about shakes the hair off your head."

"Do you think we'll have any trouble crossing the creek?" Erin asked.

"We'll know soon enough. If you listen real careful, you can hear the water."

For the first time since they'd started their trip, Jube was silent, listening to the growing sound of the water. He stopped the mules at the crest of the hill.

Lost Creek churned down below them. Muddy torrents ripped through the brush on either side of the banks, then plunged and swirled angrily downstream. Even Jube had to raise his voice to be heard above the noise.

"She's runnin' high, ain't she? Here, Preacher, you best take the mules while I git down and study on this." He handed Douglas the reins and scrambled off the wagon.

"Do you think it's safe to try and cross?" Erin asked.

Douglas looked over the water. "I don't know. The current is swift, but it isn't very wide. Anyway, this Jube seems to know what he's doing."

"But, what if the mules should stumble? The wagon might overturn, mightn't it?"

"There's no need to borrow trouble," said Douglas. "Try to be calm. I'm sure Jube won't take any unnecessary risks."

Jube climbed back up into the wagon and took the reins. "Well, best I can tell, the water's three, maybe four, foot deep out in the middle. We might git our feet wet, but I reckon we can cross."

Jube started the team and they headed down the rocky bank. The water swirled around the mules' hooves and pulled through the wheels. It rose up to the axles, then finally, it poured against the bottom of the wagon box. They had made it over halfway across when the mules stopped.

Jube slapped the reins down hard. "Git up mules! Yah! Stub-

born, rock-brained animals! Here, Preacher, take the lines again.
I'll git down and see if I can give these ornery critters a reason
to move. When I say so, give them a slap with the reins, and
don't be gentle."

Jube eased himself down hip deep into the water and got
behind the mule on the left. He waved at Douglas, and Douglas laid the reins down hard on the mules' backs. The team
flinched and rocked the wagon, but they did not move.

"Ain't no use," Jube yelled. He worked his way back to the
wagon seat. "Miz Erin, you slide over here and let me shoulder you to dry ground."

Erin started to protest, but Jube cut her off. "I ain't askin',
I'm tellin'. Now slide over 'fore the gravel starts warshin' out
from under these wheels."

"Are you sure you can carry her?" Douglas asked. "Perhaps
I should do it."

Jube stared evenly at Douglas. "I've hauled things through
these cricks since before you were in diapers, boy. You jist hold
the reins till I git her on the ground, then I'll come back for
you."

Jube balanced with one arm around Erin's back and the other
beneath her legs. He lifted her from the wagon and they started
their slow, halting walk to the bank. The sound of the water
flooded Erin's ears. She clung to Jube's vest as he braced himself against the mule's flank. For a moment, Erin feared that
they might be sucked between the animals' legs. Then the next
thing she knew, she was sitting on the creek bank.

"Miz Erin, you all right?" Jube asked. "You look a might
peaked."

"I'm fine. . .just a little shaky."

"You stay put. I'll go see about the Preacher."

Just as Jube straightened up, Erin saw Douglas jump into
the water by the side of the wagon. Douglas disappeared once,
twice, and then the current pushed him downstream. The water threw him into the roots of an upturned tree.

"Grab on to those ruts!" Jube yelled. "I'll find something to pull you out!"

Jube ran to the edge of the creek and snapped a thick branch off a wind-thrown cottonwood. He stretched the limb across the water, and after three tries, Douglas finally grasped it. Jube pulled him in, and Erin ran to help as Douglas half climbed, half stumbled up the bank.

"Are you all right, Douglas?" Erin asked.

"Yes, I think so," he gasped. "I thought I could walk out alone."

Jube was standing over them. "You fool!" he said. "I ought to knock that smile right off your face. Didn't I say to wait? What kind of ninny jumps off a wagon on the downstream side in high water, that's what I'd like to know." Jube sent a scornful stream of tobacco into the creek. "I'll go git the wagon out. You two see if you can git yourselves back over to the road."

Two red spots burned on Douglas' cheeks. "Who does that old man think he is, talking like that to me?" He started to get up, but his shoes slipped in the mud and he fell flat. Erin reached out to grab his arm, but he jerked away and struggled to his feet.

Jube had managed to coax the mules out of the water, and he stood waiting by the wagon. They were a bedraggled lot. Douglas and Jube were soaked to the skin, and Erin's new traveling suit was wrinkled and streaked with sand. Jube helped Erin back in the wagon, then Douglas climbed up beside her. Nearly an hour had passed since they had started across the creek; the afternoon shadows were long.

"Preacher, I reckon I laid my mouth on you pretty heavy back there," Jube said. "But I jist didn't want nobody hurt is all. You gotta know that we have good reasons for doing things the way we do 'round here."

"I'll try to keep that in mind in the future," Douglas said tersely. "Thank you for helping me out of the water."

"I reckon you're welcome."

About a mile from the creek Jube suddenly pulled on the reins. "Whoa, mules."

"Why are we stopping?" Douglas asked.

"Well, Preacher, if you look up ahead, you might see. That hill there's a monster, and I figure with all this folderol in the back, the mules need a rest and a running start to make it up. Truth is, the road don't flatten out much till we git to the schoolhouse. The whole way is either up or down."

The mules seemed to sense what Jube wanted them to do. After a moment's rest, they took off at a trot and pulled the wagon several yards up the hill before the grade slowed them down. Erin's back was pressed hard into the seat as they climbed up the snakebacked trail. The mules huffed loudly with each step they took. Finally, they reached a spot that was not quite so steep, and Jube let them rest. He pointed to a clearing on their right.

"That's the Witbeck cabin," he said. "If you look close, you can see it through the trees." In the twilight, Erin could just make out a small gray cabin with a stone chimney. She yawned and tried to find a more comfortable position on the wagon seat.

"You're jist about tuckered out, ain't you, Miz Erin?"

"I admit, I'll be glad to get off of this wagon."

"Well, it won't be much longer, another mile or so."

The mules were tired, too. They had slowed considerably in the last few minutes despite Jube's repeated attempts to hurry them along. Erin's head pounded with every move the wagon made. She didn't care any more what kind of home the Gillams had; all she wanted to see was a bed, any kind of bed, and the sooner the better. Douglas had given up the battle to stay awake some time ago, and his head nodded and bounced on his chest.

They came around a curve to a steep downhill stretch. Jube stopped the mules, stood up, and yelled with all his might, "Hey-hoo!"

Douglas jumped straight up in the air. "What is it?" he cried, "What's wrong?"

Jube laughed. "Nothing's wrong, Preacher. See that little portion of light there? Gillams' is right down the road. Git up, mules."

Douglas sat back in the seat. "I don't see why we had to make such a production of our arrival," he mumbled. "I feel as if we were leading a circus parade."

"Sorry if I scared you, Preacher, but it'd be smart for you to remember to give a yell before you set foot on a man's property, especially after dark. It ain't jist polite; it's a whole lot safer. Most folks here have dogs that don't like strangers."

The Gillams' house was at the bottom of the hill, where the road ended. The silhouettes of three people were in the open front door. They were a most welcome sight.

three

Someone was knocking on the door. Erin sat up in her bed and tried to focus on the source of the sound. Then, she remembered. She was at the Gillams'. A woman was calling her name.

"Erin? Erin, you awake, honey? Breakfast is ready. You best git a move on."

Erin threw her feet over the side of the bed. The voice belonged to the woman named Mattie who had greeted her the night before. Erin blinked the sleep out of her eyes, remembering that there had also been a boy with blond hair, the younger brother, Ben, whom Jube had talked about. Vaguely, she also remembered her hand being lost between the huge fingers of a very large man who had introduced himself as Tucker Gillam.

The sun had not yet risen, and Erin lit the lamp and hurried to get dressed. She thought of locating the bathroom, but since the only thing to serve those needs was out somewhere behind the house, she decided to wait. She poured some water from the pitcher on the washstand, and sponged her hands and face, while the smell of coffee and bacon hurried her along.

In the combination parlor and dining room Mattie was hovering over Douglas, filling his coffee cup and nudging dishes toward him. When Mattie saw Erin, she set the coffeepot down.

"Good morning. Are you hungry, child? You jist come on over here and set down. The other men already et, but I reckon we got enough left to fill you up."

"Thank you, Mattie," said Erin. "It looks delicious."

Douglas stood up as she came to the table. "Good morning, Erin. Did you sleep well?"

"Yes, thank you. I can't remember ever sleeping so soundly."

Douglas sat back down on the bench, and Mattie poured Erin a cup of coffee.

"You must be near starved. Like as not that punkin-headed Jube didn't feed y'all enough yesterday to keep a bird alive. I got a fresh pan of biscuits in the oven. You jist help yourself, Erin."

Mattie disappeared into the kitchen. The table was crowded with dishes of eggs and ham, red eye gravy, thick sliced bacon, biscuits, coffee, and apple pie. *Imagine,* thought Erin, *apple pie for breakfast!*

Mattie brought out a fresh plate of biscuits and sat down. "Jube told us about your trouble crossing Lost Crick. I reckon that was one baptizin' that you wasn't counting on, huh, Preacher?"

Douglas nodded but Erin noticed his smile was small and tight.

"If it hadn't for Jube, I don't know what we would have done." Erin said. "Douglas was very lucky to come out of the creek unharmed."

Mattie smiled. "'Pears to me it wasn't no luck a'tall. God had His hand on you children. It was Him who brought you through that troubled water."

"I guess I hadn't thought of it that way," Erin said.

"Well, study on it sometime. The Word says that our very hairs be numbered and that He causeth all things to work together for good to those who love Him. Ain't no need for luck when you're in the Father's hands." Mattie looked over at Douglas' plate. "Listen to me, a carryin' on while the Preacher's dish goes empty."

"Thank you, Mattie, but I'm stuffed. I couldn't eat another bite."

"Land, Preacher, then we got to git you eating like a country boy. You could use a little meat on your bones. I expect you and Miz Erin will want some time to settle in this morning. There's still one more of your satchels here that needs to go over to the cabin."

Douglas had been assigned to a cabin? He glanced at Erin, a tiny frown between his brows, but he said nothing, only excused himself to go finish unpacking.

Erin turned back toward Mattie. The older woman was short

and heavy set, an elfin butterball with a crown of white hair and twinkling blue eyes. The thing that Erin liked most, though, was the way Mattie looked when she had been talking about God.

"Now that we got rid of all the menfolks, I reckon we got jist a minute or two for us girls to git acquainted," Mattie said. "Now tell me, what made a pretty young thing like you come down here to the sticks to keep school?"

"Well. . .I don't know. It was just something I felt I needed to do. Would it seem childish to you if I said I felt that God had called me here?"

"Childish? Mercy, no! Was it childish when Moses got called up by God out of the wilderness? Surely it weren't childish for the Lord to call His disciples out of their fishin' boats. Being called is a special thing, to be took serious."

"Mattie, I have so many plans," Erin confided. "There are new ways of teaching, programs that I can hardly wait to start."

"It's a pleasure to see a young person so eager to work. You jist keep your eyes on the Master, child, and you'll do fine. And if ever you want someone to talk to, you come see old Mattie. It's a pure joy having another woman in the house."

"Thank you, Mattie, I'm sure I'll take you up on that." Erin folded her napkin and put it on the table. "Would you like some help with these dishes?" she asked.

"No, you take things easy today. If you can't find what you need, jist give me a holler." Mattie stacked the dishes and cups and went off into the kitchen.

It took several tries, but Erin finally arranged all her clothes into the wardrobe and dresser in her room. After she got her room in order, she wandered out on the front porch.

Yesterday's clouds had given way to a brilliant blue sky. It was quite some time until lunch, so Erin decided to go exploring. Erin had always loved horses, and Mattie had said she should feel free to roam, so she crossed the pasture and walked toward the barn. She turned into the open door, and suddenly, out of nowhere, a pile of filthy straw rained down over her head.

"Stop!" she cried. "Watch what you're doing!"

Tucker Gillam stepped out into the sunlight. "Well, excuse me, miss, but I'm not used to having young ladies sneak up behind me when I muck out a stall. Maybe you ought to let a person know next time you go poking your nose in someone's barn."

"I didn't know it was you, Mr. Gillam, I'm sorry. I meant no offense. Mattie told me it would be all right if I had a look around."

"No offense taken." He went on raking out the stall. "Sorry I missed you at breakfast, but farm folk have to git up early and work for a living. By the way, we ain't formal here—everybody calls me Tucker."

He pitched fresh straw into the clean stall. "You're welcome to look around here if you like," he said. "But until you figure out the difference between honey and horse manure, maybe I'd best have Ben to show you around."

"Fine, would this afternoon be convenient?"

Tucker leaned on the top of his pitchfork. "I wouldn't say it's convenient, but I believe we can spare Ben for one afternoon."

"Thank you, I'll look forward to it. Now, if you will excuse me, I think I had better go and change my clothes."

"Ma'am? You might want to wear something a little less fancy, if you have it, especially those shoes. Looks like all they'd be good for is a wrenched ankle."

Erin raised her chin a notch. "Thank you for your concern."

Tucker touched the brim of his hat and nodded his head. "See you at dinner, ma'am."

Erin turned and stepped into a pile of warm manure. Tucker's laugh was a deep rumble.

"Looks like you're gonna have to find those 'suitable' shoes a mite sooner than you thought," he said.

Erin did not reply. Instead, she walked briskly toward the house and slipped into her room. As she changed her soiled clothing, she could think of nothing but how aggravating

Tucker Gillam was. He was big and arrogant, and he looked like the orphanage bulldog. He probably was admired around Lost Creek for his size, or perhaps for his money, but Erin was determined that she would not let him intimidate her.

ﾀﾞ

As Erin sat by the window and let the breeze blow through her hair, she began to feel ashamed. She had been a missionary for less than one day, and already she had lost her temper. Mattie had said, "Just keep your eyes on the Master and you'll do fine," but keeping her eyes on God was not going to be as easy as she had thought. However, holding a grudge against Tucker was not only unchristian, she decided, it was also unwise. After all, his opinions held a lot of weight in this community.

Mattie rang the lunch bell and the men lined up at the washstand on the back porch. Erin peeked into the kitchen and saw Mattie beating a pot of mashed potatoes.

"There you are, Erin," she said. "Here, why don't you finish mashing these taters while I dish up the chicken. Men are plenty hungry by dinner time; won't do to make them wait."

Erin picked up the spoon and tried to imitate what she had seen Mattie do. Though she tried her best, pieces of potato flew over the sides of the pot and the rest stuck together in gooey clumps at the bottom.

"Erin, those taters about done?" Mattie called.

"I'm afraid I'm making a mess. They look awfully lumpy."

Mattie inspected the pot and smiled. "Sometimes, you jist got to git mean with them." She added some cream and a big dollop of butter and whipped the spoon furiously until the potatoes turned light and fluffy. "There you be, jist took a little elbow grease. Now, git that bowl on the table while I dish up the rest."

The table was laden with bowls of green beans laced with bacon, creamed corn, fresh bread, gravy, radishes, sliced onions, a molasses cake, cold buttermilk, and something called "cracklin'" cornbread. It was a far cry from the skimpy soup and bread served for luncheon at the Manchester Orphanage.

"Y'all better git in here and eat your dinner before I give it to the hogs," Mattie called out the door.

Tucker came in, followed by Jube and a man Erin did not know, then came Ben and Douglas. Mattie made the introductions as the men sat down.

"Miz Erin, this here's Clay Reynolds. He's helping us during harvest. Clay lives down the road a piece. I reckon you know the rest. Now set down 'fore it gits cold. Preacher, would you favor us by sayin' grace?"

"Certainly," Douglas said. "Shall we bow for prayer? Our most gracious heavenly Father, we thank Thee for Thy very bountiful blessings, and for this great abundance of food. We thank Thee, oh God, for the hands that prepared it. Lead us now into Thy paths of loving kindness this day. In Jesus' blessed name we pray, amen."

Everyone began to eat. Douglas and Erin watched in awe as the men stacked food high on their plates, then covered everything with gravy. Tucker poured coffee from his cup into his saucer, blew on it, and then drank directly from the saucer.

The headmistress would have much to say about country table manners, Erin thought. She searched for a topic of conversation to take her mind off their odd customs.

"Ben," she began, "Tucker said you might be willing to show Douglas and me around this afternoon."

Ben smiled broadly, and heedless of the food in his mouth, replied, "Yes'm. I'd be proud to, right after dinner."

"Jist remember to git yourself back here in time to clean that chicken house before supper," Tucker said. "And you'd best chew that food with your mouth closed, boy. We don't want our company thinking we ain't got no manners."

Tucker got up from the table and walked to the door. "Ben, you take good care of Miz Erin and the Preacher," he said. "Remember they ain't used to hard walking."

"I'm sure we'll be fine," Douglas said.

"Well, watch out for them wampus kitties," Tucker warned. Ben's eyes brightened. "Reckon I ought to take my rifle gun along, jist in case?"

"No, them wampus kitties don't usually come out before dark."

Douglas and Erin looked at each other. Could a "wampus kitty" be some kind of backwoods name for a bobcat? Or perhaps it was a name for a less than desirable member of their community. Erin made up her mind to keep a careful eye out when they went for their walk.

Ben showed them the chicken house and the pig pen, where a half dozen brown pigs were sleeping contentedly in a mud wallow. Douglas leaned on the fence and looked into the pen. "Are these all the pigs you keep?" he asked. "I thought Mr. Reynolds said something about a hog roundup."

"Oh, these hogs here is jist what we fatten up special for the family. The acorn mast they eat in the wild makes their meat bitter, so we feed 'em corn and slops for a month or two before we butcher. Tuck's got over a hundred fifty head of hogs ear-notched up in the hills."

"Ear-notched? What's that?" Erin asked.

"It's a lot like the branding they do out West, I guess. You jist cut the ear a special way when they's small—ours is under half crop, right ear—then, when we round 'em up for the market, we know whose pigs they are."

"Are the other livestock ear-notched?"

"No, ma'am, we only notch the hogs. Most folks 'round here notch cows too, but the last few years Tucker's been favoring ear tags for them and the sheep."

They walked through a grove of fruit trees. The peaches had already been picked, but the apples hung thick and red on the branches, full of promise. Ben pointed towards another building. "That there's the smoke house, and that little lean-to is jist for farm machinery." They were coming full circle to the front of the house. "The stone building that butts into the hill yonder is an icehouse, only one 'round here. We've kept ice right up to harvest some years."

"Ben, did your father build all this by himself?"

"Oh, no, ma'am. First was the homestead cabin that Grampa built, that's where Jube and the preacher sleep now. Grampa built the barn and most of the outbuildings, too. Then Pa and Grampa started on the big house. By the time I was borned, Pa and Tuck had added the second story. They built on the big kitchen and Mattie's room a couple years before Ma died."

"Your Pa must have cared very much about this land to work so hard," Erin said.

Ben kicked at the gravel in the road with his toes. "I reckon nobody could farm as good as Pa did. Tuck, he takes real good care of things, though, and pretty soon I'll be able to work a full man's share around here. I'll be thirteen my next birthday."

"It'll be a pleasure to have some older pupils like you. Are you looking forward to starting school?"

"Being truthful, ma'am, I can't say as I am. But Tuck, he gave his word to Pa that I'd git schoolin' before I was growed, and both me and Tuck are set on keeping that promise, no matter how we feel about it ourselves."

"I see. Well, I think it's very good of you both to keep your word like that, don't you, Douglas?"

"Hmm? Oh, yes, of course."

"Tuck says a man ain't nothin' if he don't keep his word." Ben looked over into the yard. "That's about all there is to see around the house. Our land covers four sections along the river. Course, not all that's planted, most of it's woods pasture. Would you like to see the river, or are you all tuckered out?"

"We're not tired!" Erin cried. "Show us the way!"

Grapevines climbed from treetop to treetop creating a shadowy canopy of leaves across the road. Ben trotted on ahead, turning back from time to time to identify a plant or animal he thought might interest his guests. He stopped by an old walnut tree. "The main road runs straight on that way, but this way's shorter, if you don't mind it being a bit upturned."

Erin smiled at Douglas. "What do you think, Reverend, can a city boy like you climb a few hills?"

Douglas rested his arm up on a tree limb. "I guess the Reverend can do anything the teacher can. Let's go, Ben."

Ben led the way to a hill so steep they had to hold on to tree roots to climb it. As Erin's skirts caught on weeds and branches, she envied the men their trousers. As Douglas and Erin gasped for breath behind him, Ben looked over his shoulder. "It ain't much further, jist one more big hill. Do you need to rest a mite?"

"No, Ben, we're fine," Erin called.

Douglas wiped his forehead with his handkerchief. "I hope you're having a wonderful adventure, Miss Corbett."

A steep hill of river gravel stretched in front of them. Each step up they took sent pebbles tumbling down. Douglas took Erin's arm to try and help her get her footing in the shifting rocks, but he was so off balance himself he nearly knocked them both over. Ben scrambled to the top first and helped pull Erin up. She was laughing so hard by then that she could hardly stand.

From their vantage point, they could see a large stretch of the Courtois River. In some places it wound lazy and flat, and in others it suddenly narrowed and plunged downstream, rushing over fallen limbs and logs only to settle down around the next bend in deep, still pools. Ben started down the bank, sending out sprays of rocks in all directions. Douglas took a step after him.

"This is awfully steep, Erin. Do you want me to help you?"

"Not only can I get down by myself, sir, but I believe that I can get there before you."

"Really? Well, I'd like to see that."

Erin half ran and half slid down the bank, putting all her weight on her down hill leg, hoping she could slow herself down before she went over the edge. Instead, she tumbled over her skirts, arms and legs flailing.

"Erin, are you all right? Are you hurt?" cried Douglas.

"Miz Corbett, you jist went a flyin'! Have you broke anything?"

She shook her head. "Nothing is too damaged except my dignity."

Relief washed over Douglas' face. "Shame on you, acting like a school girl and scaring me half to death."

Erin smiled naughtily. "I'm sorry, Douglas. But, you will have to admit, I did beat you down the hill."

"She's got you on that one, Preacher," Ben said.

Douglas sighed and shook his head. He looked at Erin for a moment and then he nodded his head as if he had decided something, though Erin could not imagine what conclusion he had reached.

For a time, they all sat on a smooth gray log and watched the river. The water was as clear as glass, each rock glistening in the riverbed like a facet in a huge, liquid diamond. Ben showed Erin the minnows, some tiny and brown, and the larger ones with red dots on their heads. They listened to the deep bass "garumph!" of the bullfrogs while blue dragonflies buzzed around their faces. Sitting there and listening, Erin discovered a calmness she had never known before.

Ben finally broke the spell. "I reckon maybe we better walk down and take the road. It's a tetch farther, but it's easier traveling."

They walked along the river bank and soon came to the log bridge that was part of the back road to the farmhouse.

"Those black-eyed Susans are so pretty. May I stop and pick some?" Erin asked.

"Surely, ma'am, but if you and the Preacher can find your own way back, I'd better be going on. It's gittin' late, and Tuck'll skin me for sure if I don't git that coop cleaned out. The house is jist a ways straight down the road."

"I'm sure we can find it," Douglas said. "You go on ahead."

Ben trotted on toward the house. Erin climbed off the road-bed to reach the flowers at the bottom of a little hill. Douglas started to follow, and Erin was suddenly aware that she and Douglas were quite alone, unchaperoned.

"Douglas," she said. "Would you mind picking some of those

red flowers over there? They would look lovely with these yellow ones."

Douglas obligingly crossed to the other side of the road while Erin struggled with the bristly flower stems. She walked back into the shadows of a cedar grove to pick some particularly bright blooms, but just as she reached down, someone pushed by her and ran deeper into the woods.

Her scream brought Douglas running, but she was already climbing back up to the road when he found her.

"What's wrong? Was it an animal?"

"No. . .a man." She couldn't seem to catch her breath. "He ran right past me."

"What did he look like?"

"I don't know. I was so surprised, I guess I didn't really look at him."

"Well, it's all right now. It was probably some local boy prowling around in the trees. I imagine you scared him as much as he scared you." Douglas looked over his shoulder. "Let's get back to the house."

Tucker, Jube, and Clay were standing in a tight circle by the fireplace when they walked in. Jube's voice rose above the rest.

"That river weren't high enough to float two cows downstream," he said. "You know them heifers jist didn't lose theirselves without a trace."

Tucker looked up as Erin and Douglas came into the room. "Miz Erin," he said, "you look like you seen a haunt. Didn't Ben listen about not tiring you out?"

Douglas pulled out a chair for her. "Erin had a little scare," he said. "She was off to the side of the road picking flowers and some hooligan hiding in the trees jumped past her and ran into the woods."

Tucker looked at her sharply. "Did you git a look at him, Miz Erin?"

"No, he ran by too fast. You don't think it could be one of those 'wampus kitties' you mentioned earlier, do you?"

The men threw back their heads and laughed. "No, ma'am,"

Tucker said. "I can jist about guarantee that it weren't no wampus kitty."

"Miz Erin," Jube said, "wampus kitties is jist something that goes bump in the dark. Ain't no natural critter by that name."

Erin glared at Tucker. He grinned back at her, but then, his smile faded. "I'd be obliged if you'd show me where you found your wampus kitty," he said. "I'm a mind to wonder if that kitty might know something about our missing cows."

four

Erin slept fitfully during the night, awakened again and again by an intense itching that burned and spread. Finally, she got out of bed, lit the lamp, and pulled up her chemise to take a closer look. Ugly red bumps lined her hips, and on the back of her right thigh was a small black spot that wouldn't come off when she rubbed it. As she puzzled over it, she heard a noise in the hall, and then a knock on the door.

"Erin? It's about time to git up." Mattie opened the door and saw Erin standing by the lamp. "Why, you're sure up early for a city gal."

"Mattie, would you look at this? I think I have some sort of rash. It itches terribly."

Mattie came over to the light and inspected her. "You got more of these—say where your drawers lie around your ankles and on your legs?"

"Yes. And on my arms, too. Do you know what it is?"

"You ain't got no rash, honey, you jist got chiggers."

"Chiggers? What is that?"

"They're a lot like skeeters, only they be tinier with no wings. They lay low in the brush and hop on when people go by. They itch like the devil, but they ain't nothing serious."

Erin pulled her wrapper back off her leg. "What about this? I can't get it off."

"Oh, now that there's a tick. A tick's a little blood suckin' bug. He's got his head good and buried in you, too."

"You mean it's alive?" Erin squirmed to get a better look.

Mattie chuckled. "Don't worry, child, we'll git him out. Hand me a match."

Mattie took the match and lit it, then blew it out and stuck the hot head on the tick; with her thumbnail and fingernail, she picked the insect off Erin's skin. "There. I'll git some salve for those chiggers and something to clean that tick bite. Next

31

time you go out trampin' in the brush, you git some penny-royal from the garden and crush it real good, then rub it on your arms and legs. That'll keep some of those critters off. Now, don't look so addlepated. Ticks and chiggers are jist a part of living in this country. You'll git used to it by and by."

Mattie's salve helped a little, but as Erin went into the dining room she still felt as if little bugs were crawling on her, and she smelled vaguely of bacon grease. Mattie set the last platter on the breakfast table, and Tucker reached for a biscuit and slathered it with apple butter.

"Preacher, you about ready to see where you're gonna hold church?" he asked.

"The schoolhouse? Yes, I was going to ask if perhaps Erin and I could see it today."

"I got a little time this morning, so I thought I'd finish the railing on the steps over there. We been planning a pie supper for Saturday night. I was thinking you might want to fix up the place a bit for folks to see. It might git 'em fired up if they saw all them fancy books setting out and ready to go."

"That is an excellent idea," said Douglas. "Erin and I should be able to get things ready in a few days' time. Don't you think so, Erin?"

"Certainly. Are our supplies already at the school?"

Tucker poured his coffee in his saucer to cool. "Yes'm. We hauled in four fair-sized crates from the mission board last month, all full of books and maps and such."

"Wonderful," Douglas said. "Erin and I shall be ready to accompany you immediately after breakfast."

After Erin helped finish clearing the table, she went out on the porch and found Douglas scratching his back against a post.

"Chiggers?" she asked.

He turned around, surprised. "Oh, Erin, excuse me." He smiled ruefully. "Are you still enjoying your adventure?"

"Of course! A few little insects won't dampen my enthusiasm."

"Well, they've dampened mine, at least until I saw you at breakfast this morning. Your dress is most becoming."

"Be careful," Erin teased. "Or you will turn my head."

"Would that be such a bad idea?"

Tucker rounded the corner, lumber and tool box in hand. "You two gonna lollygag all day, or you coming with me?"

"Aren't we taking a wagon?" Erin asked.

"It's only a mile or so, but if you don't think you can walk it..."

"Of course I can. I only wondered since you were carrying those boards and tools."

"Aw, they ain't nothing for a working man."

Erin handed Douglas the picnic basket Mattie had packed for them, and they started up the hill. Squirrels chattered angrily at them for disturbing their peace, and tan grasshoppers snapped away from their feet.

"Preacher, I hear you're all the way from Chicago," Tucker said.

"That is my home, but I have spent the past few years at seminary in Kentucky."

"Ain't that something, all the way from Kentuck. What in thunder brings a high falutin' man like yourself to these woods?"

"Well, my father is also a pastor and he thought perhaps this would be a good experience for a young minister like myself."

"Ma always said the first pancake of the morning was likely to be burnt around the edges. Is that what you're meaning, Preacher?"

"I suppose you could put it that way. We felt that this would be an appropriate place for me to smooth off the rough corners, so to speak."

Tucker shifted the load on his shoulder and looked over at Douglas. "You mean, it don't matter so much if you make a mistake here, it being a woodsy church, and you gitting paid by the mission board instead of by the people."

Douglas looked uncomfortable. "Of course it matters, but you are right, this particular position is of little risk to me. I would want you to know, however, that I will hardly get rich on the fifteen dollars a month the mission board pays. I certainly am not here for the money."

"I'm right proud to hear that, Preacher. But I'd have you to know that fifteen dollars cash money is more'n some folks around here see in a year, so if I were you, I'd keep the particulars of my earnings to myself."

"Thank you," Douglas said stiffly. "I'll keep that in mind."

Tucker turned his attention to Erin. "What about you, Miz Erin, you here for experience or—what did I hear the Preacher call it?—you here for an adventure?"

So he had been listening to their conversation on the porch!

"I should hope to gain experience from any teaching position I accept," Erin replied. "And yes, I am quite excited about this assignment and about learning the ways of the people here. It is an adventure of sorts."

"Even when it comes with cow patties and chiggers?"

"Yes, even then, and I find it most indelicate of you to discuss such things."

"Yes'm, I reckoned you would." Tucker pointed up toward the top of the hill. "School's jist past that bend on the hilltop."

Erin hurried on ahead of the men, glad to have an excuse to get away from Tucker. "This is my school," she thought as she went inside the small, plain building. Her heart filled with joy. Soon, these desks would be filled with pupils eager to learn about everything in the world, and she would be their teacher.

Douglas had followed her inside, but Tucker remained in the doorway. "Reckon this'll do?" he asked.

"Yes, it will do just fine," Erin said. "I could use some water from the pump so I can start cleaning up."

"Bucket's in the corner," said Tucker.

Douglas hesitated, then he picked up the pail. "Of course," he said. "I will be right back."

Tucker watched as Douglas went out the back door. "He ain't exactly zealous about work, is he?"

Erin sat down in one of the pupils' desks. "You don't like us very much, do you, Tucker?"

Tucker reached one hand up and rested it on the top of the door frame. "That's matter of fact and to the point, ain't it? Truth is, it ain't a matter of liking or not liking you, Miz Erin. I got a little brother I promised to git schooled. If some religion comes along in the bargain, fine and dandy, that's the way Pa wanted it. But I want a teacher that's for certain sure gonna stay around more'n a couple weeks, and the last thing we need is a dude preacher who come to do his little thing until he can get a big church in the city."

"I think you are judging Douglas too harshly. He hasn't even had a chance to begin his ministry yet. He isn't afraid of hard work either, he just isn't accustomed to rural life."

"No, I expect he's not, but if he wants folks to pay him any mind, he might should learn."

"Douglas and I will both learn, Tucker. I made a commitment to teach here, and I intend to do so."

"You're a pretty young lady, and I got nothing against you personal, but you ain't got a notion of what you're gitting into. Speakin' frankly, I think the first time this job gits hard or dirty, and it will, you'll be gone on the first wagon you can git out of here."

"Is that so! Well, I'm afraid you'll be sorely disappointed next spring when I lead our school in closing exercises."

"Not disappointed, jist surprised." Tucker picked up his toolbox. "I best git this railing finished. There's chores to do back at the house."

Tucker left shortly after dinner, having finished his work on the stairs. Douglas and Erin spent the rest of the day cleaning and unpacking. At the bottom of the first crate, Erin found a round-bodied spider with the longest, thinnest legs she had ever seen. She quickly pulled her hand out of its path as it scurried up the side of the packing box. "What sort of creature is that?"

Douglas turned the crate on its side and smashed the spider with his shoe. "I don't know," he said. "I'm afraid we didn't study much entomology in seminary."

"Speaking of seminary, did they teach you how to go about building a church?"

Douglas took a deep breath and let it out slowly. "Well, there are several programs I studied in school that could be implemented. My first priority will be to raise the quality of their church services. I am told that most backwoods churches have only a very rudimentary concept of formal worship. Then, I'll begin laying the organizational groundwork, setting up committees for Sunday School and special programs to increase attendance, and so forth."

"But, Douglas, I thought we were sent here to tell people about the Gospel. What if they don't want to change the way they worship?"

Douglas looked at Erin as if he were explaining something to a child. "I didn't mean to imply that the Gospel was not central to what we teach—but there is much more to mission work than that. I've had the privilege of a fine education and it is my duty to lift these people to a higher level of understanding."

"I hadn't thought of it like that," she said. "I'm afraid I don't know much about being a missionary."

"Don't worry, Erin, you will be fine."

The locusts were humming their afternoon song by the time the second crate was emptied. "I move we wait until tomorrow to open the next one," Douglas said.

"I'll second that motion. I need to borrow a broom and some rags from Mattie before I can clean this place properly anyway."

"Then I suggest we find our way home."

Douglas opened the door and the afternoon sunlight angled into the classroom. A gentle breeze whispered through the leaves and sent brownish-gray lizards skittering away from the warm sunlight where they had laid basking in the warm dust beside the school. Erin moved to stand beside Douglas in the doorway.

He turned his head toward her. "You're a lovely young woman, Erin Corbett."

"Thank you. Douglas, but I don't feel lovely, I'm covered with dust and cobwebs."

Douglas shut the door behind them, and together they walked to the road. He picked up a pine cone and threw it down the hill ahead of them. "Erin, we're going to be working closely together, so I think we should be honest with one another, shouldn't we?"

"Yes, of course."

"If we were still in society, I would send you little gifts and take you to dinners. But it's different here. I realize we've just recently met, but I am a man who knows what he wants, and I'm generally used to getting it. If you would agree, I would like permission to court you."

Erin looked down at the road, trying to slow her thoughts. "I believe I would like that, Douglas, but . . ."

"But what?"

"Well, for one thing, I don't think anyone else should know. There will be too many times like today when we'll be working together alone. People would misunderstand if they thought there was anything between us. It would damage the ministry."

"You're right, of course," he said. "Very well, we will keep it a secret for now, and I promise to be on my best behavior, even when we are alone."

Erin stopped to look down from the hilltop. The trees formed a lush green carpet which covered ridge upon sculptured ridge of rugged land. "Look, Douglas, isn't that beautiful? 'I will lift up eyes unto the hills, from whence cometh my help. My help cometh from the Lord, which made heaven and earth.'"

Douglas stood quietly behind her. "Psalm 121."

"Yes. It's been my favorite since I was a little girl. God is going to bless this work, Douglas. It is going to be successful, you'll see."

"Well, if it isn't, it won't be from lack of trying on your part, Erin. Let's get back to the house before I am tempted to break my promise."

five

"It's no use, Mattie. Your pie looks delicious, but mine looks as if the crust were made of cowhide."

Mattie chuckled. "Yours does look a little cattywampus, but it ain't bad for a first try."

"Maybe not, but I don't want to take this sad thing to the pie supper."

Mattie thought a moment. "Might be that I got a way to fix that. Suppose after we fancy up our boxes, you put your name in my box and I'll put my name in yours, then we'll carry our own pies in to the schoolhouse."

"That wouldn't be honest, would it?"

"Oh, honey, you jist don't understand about pie suppers. Why, most of the fun is the gals trying t'fool the menfolks. Anything's fair! The young bucks git theirselves worked up in a terrible lather guessing which pie is their sweetie's, and then they try to bid everybody else out."

Erin looked down at her lop-sided creation. "But you wouldn't want people to think you baked this mess."

"Child, I've lived 'round here these sixty years. Folks know I'm generally a good enough cook. It's no skin off my teeth if they hear I made up one bad pie. Anyhow, what I had in mind was to play a little foolery on Jube. That old coot's been aggravating me for nigh on to fifteen years now. He puts the high bid on my pies and then I'm obliged to spend the rest of the evening listening to his gabble. This way I can have the fun of pulling his leg a little—if you don't mind spending some time with the old buzzard."

"I don't mind."

"You best git changed then. I'll finish up these boxes."

Back in her room, Erin looked over her clothes in the wardrobe. She was tired of the plain work dresses she had been wearing for the past few days. She decided her white lawn

38

would do nicely for a special occasion like a pie supper. They were to ride in the wagon, so she gladly put her low-heeled boots away and pulled out a pair of kid slippers. There was no reason, Erin decided, to look dowdy just because she was a missionary. She twisted her hair up high, inserted a horn comb, and pinned on a small straw hat, tilting it far forward. She looked in the mirror with satisfaction.

Erin was pleased when the men stopped talking as she entered the room. Douglas stood up and walked toward her.

"Erin, you are a refreshing sight," he said. "Won't you make an impression on the community tonight!"

Tucker cleared his throat. "Oh, she'll do that for sure, like a peacock in a chicken house. Where did a gal grown up in an orphanage get such folderol?"

"I earned it," said Erin. "I've worked afternoons and Saturdays in a millinery shop since I was fourteen."

Ben scowled at Tucker. "I think she's real pretty," he said. "I ain't never seen such fancy wearin' clothes."

"I never said she wasn't pretty," Tucker replied. "We'd best git on the wagon if you want to be there in time to vote for the beauty cake."

Mattie and Erin loaded their pies, then Tucker helped Mattie onto the wagon seat, while Douglas, Ben, and Erin found places on the fresh straw in the wagon bed. Tucker spoke to the horses and they trotted up the hill.

"Mattie," Erin asked, "What is a 'beauty cake'?"

"Oh, that's the money-makin'est part of a pie supper. Somebody bakes a cake, and the boys pay a penny a vote to pick the prettiest girl there. The girl with the most votes wins the beauty cake, and she shares it with them that voted for her. A good pie might bring a quarter or so, but the beauty cake can run as high as three or four dollars." Mattie rubbed her broad forehead. "Whilst I study on it, Preacher, I reckon you know that it wouldn't be fitting for you to make any bids tonight, especially on the beauty cake. Folks 'round here jist wouldn't confidence a courtin' preacher."

Douglas coughed nervously. "I had not thought of it like that," he said. "I'll try to see that I am nothing more than an interested spectator."

They rounded the corner and drove into the schoolyard, where Jube greeted them and made his way to Mattie's side of the wagon. "Need some help with them pies, do ya, Mattie?"

"You leave them pies be, old man, and mind your business. Erin and I can manage without your help. If you're jist burning to do a good deed, why don't you take the Preacher around and let him meet the menfolks."

Jube spat on the ground. "All right, old woman, you don't have to be so tetchous. Some folks jist don't have no natural kindness in them."

Erin and Mattie picked up their pies and started toward the schoolhouse. Barefoot children scooted around the woods near the edge of the yard. Douglas and Jube joined a group of men assembled by the pump. From the coins they were exchanging, Erin assumed that they must be voting for the beauty cake.

There were a half dozen or so women clustered around the platform inside the school. Erin quickly realized, to her embarrassment, that most of the ladies were wearing the plainest of dresses, and only a few even wore shoes.

Mattie turned back toward Erin. "Well, c'mon, child," she said. "Don't jist stand and gawk, they ain't gonna bite you." She called to the other women, "Becky, Liza, all of you, come and meet the new teacher." Mattie motioned to a matronly lady standing next to a girl who looked to be about the same age as Erin. "Miz Erin Corbett, this here's the Widder Puckett and her daughter Bessie, and there's Carrie Witbeck, and this is Becky Keller, and Liza Reynolds. That's Lela Stiles, and her daughter-in-law, Rose. Rose and Emmit jist got married last spring."

"Congratulations, Rose," Erin said. "It is so nice to meet you all. I hope to get to know you all better soon."

Obviously, the Widow and her daughter were the fashion conscience for the community. While not elaborately dressed by city standards, their clothes were more stylish than the other women's, and their hats overflowed with feathers and ribbon. The Widow eyed Erin's and Mattie's pastries.

"Why, Miz Corbett, did you make a pie too?" she exclaimed. "Ain't it a wonder, a city gal who can cook."

"Well, actually," Erin stuttered, "I didn't. . ."

"City gals got to eat too, don't they?" said Mattie. "Shouldn't be no wonder that Erin knows how to cook."

The Widow pulled herself erect and peered down at Erin. "That's a beautiful dress you're wearing, Miz Corbett. Ain't nobody here seen such a fancy fine outfit. Looks like you came right off a Bazaar fashion plate."

"Why, thank you, Mrs. Puckett."

"Course," Mrs. Puckett continued, "some folks might say such truck ain't fittin' a gal who's given to be a missionary, but I'm more broad-minded than most. With a daughter like Bessie, here, I understand how much young gals like to dress in Sunday go-to-meetin' clothes. Bessie don't have no need of real fancy dresses, though, she being so naturally pretty. She's won the beauty cake two years in a row, you know."

"Really?" Erin said. "How nice. I wish you luck tonight, Bessie."

Bessie and her mother smiled identical toothy smiles and excused themselves. Mattie leaned close to Erin as they walked away. "Now, don't you pay her no mind," she whispered. "Naomi Puckett's been puttin' on airs 'round here for years. She's jist afraid you might outshine that daughter of hers."

There was a commotion in the yard as an odd little wagon pulled up in front of the door. The bottom half was a common farm rig, but a box house had been built over the bed with a door in back and a sloped roof on top. A man in a worn black suit and a wide-brimmed hat was driving. Next to him sat a rather unkempt looking young man.

Mattie peered out of the window. "Looks like Brother Butler got hisself here," she said.

Mattie had told Erin a little about him. Since last winter he had been the circuit preacher. Each week he traveled to one of four different congregations in Washington County and held meetings on Saturdays and Sundays. Now that Douglas had arrived, Reverend Butler's services were no longer required at Lost Creek Mission. To soften the loss of one of the Reverend's more profitable churches, the community had planned this pie supper. All the money raised was to go to Reverend Butler as a love offering.

The women made their way out of the schoolhouse to greet "Brother Silas" and gather their children together for the start of the pie auction. Erin found Douglas, and they watched Reverend Butler work his way through the crowd, shaking hands and hugging children as he went.

"Evening, Brother Silas," called Mrs. Stiles. "Did Winifred come with you?"

"No, bless the Lord, that girl done twisted her ankle gitting water from the crick. I thought she best rest it."

"Well, tell your daughter we asked after her."

"I will, Miz Stiles, thank you kindly." Reverend Butler stopped and looked in Douglas' direction. "How do, stranger. You must be the new college preacher they brought on, bless the Lord."

"Yes, sir, I'm Douglas Teterbaugh, and this is Erin Corbett."

Reverend Butler nodded to Erin and shook Douglas' hand. He removed his hat and wiped his oily forehead on his sleeve. "Well, bless the Lord, I'm an honest man, and I want you to know that they ain't no hard feelings about you coming in here and taking over my church. I jist praise the Lord that the folks will have regular preachin' every Sunday."

Reverend Butler surveyed the group in the school yard. "You won't mind, though, if I go ahead with the protracted meetings. It's already been spread around that I'll be preaching God's Word twice a day, for a whole week over on the riverbank, starting a week from next Monday."

"Well, no. . .of course not," said Douglas. "I wouldn't want to interfere with something that has already been planned."

"That's fine, jist fine. If you've a mind to, brother, I'd be proud for you to give the afternoon sermon at the meetings. Proper protracted meetings has at least two preachers, after all."

Erin could see that Douglas was struggling to be diplomatic. "Thank you, Reverend," he said. "But I think I'll do well to get started with the work here at the mission."

Reverend Butler looked off into the woods, then stared back at Douglas. "Well, do what you think best. I can understand a young preacher boy not being able yet to speak more'n once a week. It'll come, son, it'll come."

Reverend Butler passed on by and went into the schoolhouse. Douglas said nothing, but Erin could tell by the flush in his cheeks that he was angry.

The boy who had ridden in with the Reverend still leaned sullenly against the wagon. "Jube," Erin asked, "who is that young man who came with Reverend Butler?"

"That'd be Butler's son, Enlo. The Preacher's had a time with that one. Seems he's always into some kind of devilment."

"Douglas, maybe we should go introduce ourselves," Erin said. Douglas nodded and took her arm. As they got closer, Erin realized just how tall the boy was. Tucker Gillam was about the only man she had seen in Lost Creek who out-sized him.

"How do you do, Enlo. I'm Douglas Teterbaugh. Jube tells me you are Reverend Butler's son."

Enlo stayed slouched against the wagon, ignoring Douglas' outstretched hand. "Well, ain't that nice," he said. "The new preacher coming over here special jist to meet me. And who is this pretty lady here? Ain't you gonna meet us up?"

"Certainly. Enlo, this is Miss Corbett."

"It's good to meet you, Enlo."

Enlo slowly looked Erin over from head to toe. "I ain't never confidenced schoolin' much, but seeing as you're the teacher, I reckon maybe I ought to study on it. I never seen such fancy gee gaws, ear bobs and everything." Enlo scratched his head and turned to Douglas. "How about it, Preacher, do you git a little sugar on the side from Teacher now and then?"

Douglas' face turned scarlet. "Young man, unless you

apologize to Miss Corbett immediately, I shall have to ask you to leave."

"You best be able to make me then, Preacher," said Enlo. He took a step toward Erin and smiled. "You think I should take up books, pretty teacher?"

Enlo's breath reeked of liquor. Douglas put his hand on the young man's shoulder and pulled him away from Erin. "I think you had better go, Enlo," he said.

Enlo's eyes narrowed; he pushed Douglas' hand away and shoved him violently to the ground. To Erin's horror, Enlo pulled a knife from his boot and held the tip to Douglas' chest. Douglas sat as if he were frozen to the ground.

The double click of a shotgun made everyone's head turn toward Tucker. The gun rested easily on his hip, but it was pointed directly at Enlo. "Drop it down, boy," he said quietly. Enlo reluctantly tossed the knife on the ground. Douglas scrambled to his feet.

"I will not have you talking to Miss Corbett like that," Douglas said.

"You make a big sound now that Tucker's gun is behind you, Preacher," Enlo replied.

Tucker set the gun down and walked toward Enlo. "You let your mouth run off in front of Miz Corbett, did you, boy?"

"I never meant nothing," Enlo said nervously. "I reckon I jist had me a little too much blue ruin."

"You know better than to come here drinking. But, drunk or sober, you best memorize this: if I hear you say one ugly word around Miz Corbett again, I'll show you a little frolic you won't soon forget."

Reverend Butler elbowed his way to the front of the crowd. He grabbed his son by the collar and pushed him up against the wagon. "You shamed me here in front of my people. You grieve me, boy. Now, you light a shuck out to the house, or I'll whup the devil out of you, here and now." Reverend Butler pushed his son in the direction of the road.

Enlo picked up his knife and put it back in his boot. "All

right," he drawled. "But, don't you think this is done between us, Preacher, not by a long shot." Enlo stumbled down the hill and disappeared into the woods.

Reverend Butler faced the crowd. "He's a prodigal and a sorrow to my heart. I'm grieving for his meanness to you, Miz Corbett. I'd take it as a special kindness if you'd still let him come to your school. I reckon he's a mite older than most in your class, but we ain't never lived no where for him to git book learned."

Erin was none too anxious to have Enlo as a pupil, but under the circumstances she could hardly refuse. "There's no harm done," she said. "If Enlo wants to learn, of course he'll be welcome."

"Ain't it about time to git this pie supper started?" Tucker asked. "Where's Jube?"

"I'm right here! Ladies and gents, if you'll bring yourselves inside the schoolhouse, we'll git her going."

❧

By the time Douglas and Erin went inside, the "married" pies had already been bought by their respective spouses and the main attraction of the evening was about to begin. Douglas and Erin found a place by Ben and Tucker near the front of the platform.

Jube held up an elaborately decorated basket with organdy bows. "Now, gents, you take a look at this fine piece of work. Looks like a good one to me. What's my bid for this pie?"

"Ten cents!" came a call from the back. Another young man bid fifteen, then the price went to twenty-five. Out of the blue, Douglas raised his hand and bid fifty cents.

"Douglas!" Erin whispered. "You aren't supposed to bid on any pies. What are you doing?"

"Don't worry, that's the Widow Puckett's pie. I heard one of the boys warn a friend not to bid on it. By purchasing her pie, I not only please the most prominent woman in my new church, but I also make a sizable gesture of good will toward Reverend Butler by contributing to his love offering." Douglas seemed very pleased with himself.

The next pie must have belonged to the girl on Erin's right, because she blushed bright red when she saw who had won the bid. Soon, only Mattie's pie and Erin's were left. Jube picked up the pie that Mattie had carried in and held it up high. Erin wondered how he would manage to bid on the pie, when he was the auctioneer.

"All right, boys, right here we have a fine lookin' parcel, apple by the smell. . .what'll I hear for it?"

Tucker raised his hand. "Ten cents," he said.

Ben looked up at his brother in surprise. "You biddin' on a pie, Tucker? Since when?"

"Hush up. I'm jist doin' Mattie a favor. She asked me to bid on her pie so she wouldn't have to set with Jube all night."

Erin could feel herself flushing. What would Tucker do when he found out her name was on that pie? The price went up to thirty cents, but Tucker won the final bid. Erin would have to spend the evening with Tucker Gillam. She couldn't understand why Jube hadn't made a bid.

Jube held up the last pie. "Folks, this ain't exactly playing by the rules, but to tell you truthful, I took a little peek and I know who belongs to this pie. I'm willing to pay forty cents for it. Is there anybody of a mind to top my price? Going once, twice, sold! Now, Miz Mattie, you jist spread out the cloth, and I'll be there to set with you directly."

The crowd laughed and applauded. Ben poked a confused Tucker in the ribs. "Reckon you got mixed up on which one was Mattie's."

"Wipe that silly grin off your face, boy," said Tucker.

Jube held up the pie with Erin's name on it. "Tucker, looks like you git to share a pie with our new school teacher."

Tucker's face showed no particular emotion. He nodded to Jube and then looked down at Erin. "Miz Erin, soon as we git done here, I'll lay us a blanket out yonder by the wagon."

Erin turned back toward Jube to hear how everyone else had been paired off. Douglas took her arm and leaned toward her ear. "I didn't know you were entering a pie, Erin," he whispered.

"It seemed like the right idea at the time," replied Erin. "Besides, it is for a good cause."

"Of course. I was just surprised, that's all."

Jube finished reading off the pairs and then it was time to announce the winner of the beauty cake. "Everyone, listen up," he called. "We had us a close one tonight. Second place for the beauty cake goes to our new school teacher, Miz Corbett, with four dollars and sixty-two cents' worth of votes. Ain't she a pretty sight?" The crowd applauded, and Erin felt her face turning red again.

"Hold on now," Jube said. "One young gal got an even five dollars' worth of votes. Our winner for the third straight year is Bessie Puckett. We've had us a fine night. We raised thirteen dollars and forty-seven cents for Brother Butler's love offering."

Silas Butler stepped up onto the platform and took hold of the lapels of his suit coat. "Brother Jube, I jist want to say a glory be and thank you to everyone here tonight. Remember me in your prayers and don't forgit the brush arbor meetings coming up. There'll be a star in your crown for helping this poor old preacher. Lord keep you all until we meet again."

Tucker picked up Erin's basket and escorted her out into the schoolyard. He spread the blanket beneath an oak tree near the well. "Be careful where you set. I wouldn't want you to git that fancy go-to-meetin' dress all dirty."

"It is painfully obvious to me that I have overdressed for this occasion, Tucker. Please don't make it worse."

"Fair enough, why don't you cut us a slab of that pie?"

He watched while she got plates and a knife out of the basket and served him a generous slice. After a few bites he put down his plate and looked at her. "Miz Erin, can you answer me a question?"

"I'll try."

"How is it your name got in the box with Mattie's pie?"

"How do you know this isn't my pie?"

"Well, for one thing, I've ate Mattie's pies since I was jist a boy, and I know Mattie didn't bake that sorry thing I saw sittin' next to this one on the table back home." Tucker grinned. "If you was wanting to eat pie with me so bad, why didn't you jist say so?"

"Mr. Gillam, it was certainly not my desire to dine with you!"

"Who was you wanting to 'dine' with then?"

"As a matter of fact, it was supposed to be Jube. Mattie said Jube always bid on her pies, and since my pie came out rather badly, she offered to switch, assuming Jube would bid on the one she carried in. She wanted to play a joke on Jube."

Tucker picked up his plate and laughed. "That Mattie. She asked me to bid on this pie to keep Jube from pestering her all night, knowing all along your name was in the basket. She's been at me for years to be more sociable. I reckon this was her way to make me do it."

"Then none of this really had anything to do with Jube?"

"Mattie still got her joke on Jube, all right."

"How is that? Jube's with Mattie. He got what he wanted."

"Yes'm, but he has to eat your pie."

Erin smiled. "I'll have to admit, it was a disaster. I do want you to know, though, that I had no intention of getting us paired together tonight."

"Don't fret about it. I reckon I know who you'd rather be paired up with." Tucker helped himself to a second piece of pie. "Your preacher friend ain't much of a hand at defending himself, is he?"

"Douglas stood up for me. Enlo was very rude."

"I don't doubt it; the boy was lickered up. If I hadn't stepped in, Enlo likely would've carved the Preacher's ears off."

"We don't know that. Anyway, Douglas is a minister. Surely you don't expect him to brawl in the dirt."

"Don't matter what I think, but that's what some folks will expect of him, if it's called for. Fine words and a glad hand might work in the city, but this is rough country. It takes a firm way to git folks' respect."

"I'm sure Douglas can do whatever is necessary."

"Maybe. What about you? You reckon you can handle Enlo and his kind at the school?"

Erin looked straight into Tucker's eyes. "I'm quite capable of teaching a class full of children, Mr. Gillam. Just because I attended an orphanage school doesn't mean my education was second best. My teaching certificate is as good as anyone's."

"Never meant to say it wasn't. I only want you to think on what you're getting yourself into, is all."

In the twilight, people began loading up their wagons and preparing to leave. Douglas came walking toward the Gillam wagon, sandwiched tightly between Widow Puckett and her daughter.

"Tucker? Tucker Gillam?" the widow called.

Tucker stood up. "Evenin', Widder. Did you enjoy the supper?"

"My yes, the Preacher's been fine company for us, telling us about all the big cities he's lived in and going to seminary and all. I think we got us a good one here. Tucker, I was wondering if you'd favor me by stopping at the house and bringing down a sack of chicken feed from the barn rafters. I must be gitting absent-minded. I never noticed we was about out, and Emmit Stiles don't come by to do my heavy work until day after tomorrow."

"I'd sure like to oblige you," Tucker said. "But I was fixing to carry the Kellers home." A light twinkled in Tucker's eyes. "I expect the Kellers wouldn't mind waiting, but since the Preacher's right here, maybe he could help you."

Douglas paused only long enough to give Tucker an irritated look. "I'd be happy to assist you, Mrs. Puckett."

"Ain't you kind," beamed Mrs. Puckett. "It won't take but a minute, we live jist up the road on Gobbler's Knob. Mayhaps you'd like to rest some in the parlor before you go. My Bessie's a fair hand at playing our pianny. It's the only one around these parts that I know of."

The Widow's voice trailed off down the road as she and Bessie hustled Douglas off. Tucker started across the school yard.

"Where are you going?" Erin asked.

Tucker smiled sheepishly. "To tell Asa Keller that I'm fixing to drive him home."

Mrs. Keller insisted on riding in the back of the wagon, even though Erin urged her to ride on the seat. Noah and Walter quickly settled in by their mother, and Mr. Keller handed little Beth up and scrambled in behind her. Mattie had decided against riding home and was planning instead to walk with Ben and the Reynolds. Erin's first impulse was to walk along with Mattie, but the thought of even a mile on that rocky road in her high-heeled slippers made a wagon ride, even a wagon ride with Tucker, sound very nice.

With no mounting block to step up on, Erin was clumsy at getting into the seat of the buckboard. She was still fumbling with her skirts when Tucker grasped both her arms and whisked her up onto the wagon. He climbed across her, released the brake, and they were off.

Too soon, they arrived at the cut off to the Keller farm. Asa insisted on walking his family in rather than taking Tucker's wagon over the rutted path in the dark.

Now that Tucker and Erin were alone, Erin wished she had walked home with Mattie, high heels or not. The wagon seat seemed too narrow with Tucker and her on it. No matter how she positioned herself, their shoulders kept brushing together.

As they continued, it dawned on her that they were going in the wrong direction. "Aren't we going to turn around?" she asked.

"No place to turn here in the dark, leastways not without chancing a wheel going down in the gully. Closest turnaround is still a half mile off. By then, it'll be quicker to take the back road across the bridge. You've never been this way, have you?"

"No. I've only seen the way Jube brought us in."

"It's a pretty road by day. There's persimmon trees and dogwood and redbud all through here. Paw paws and sassafras, too." Tucker urged the horses to pick up the pace. "You still mad about me setting the Widder Puckett on the Preacher?"

"It was on purpose, wasn't it? I thought any woman who runs her own farm could manage to get a little sack of feed down for her chickens."

"That shows how much you know, Miss. We don't git to the store every little bit 'round here. No, the Widder was tellin' the truth. That feed sack weighs upwards of a hundred pounds."

"I'm sorry. I didn't realize."

Tucker laughed. "'Course, you're probably right. I'd bet my left foot that the Widder has plenty of feed put back somewheres. She loves them old hens too much to let them go hungry. I reckon she's got the Preacher in her parlor jist about now, and they're listening to Bessie bang out a piece on the pianny."

"It wasn't very nice to force Douglas into a situation like that."

"Maybe not, but it's better him than me, and if he's gonna be a preacher, he's got to git used to visiting. Besides, I kindly thought he had it coming, buying the Widder's pie jist so he could git in good with her like he did."

Erin didn't want to admit it, but he was right on both counts. She supposed one evening with the Pucketts wouldn't do Douglas any harm.

The sweet night air eased down around their shoulders like a comfortable old quilt. The frogs and crickets and hoot owls each sang their part in serenade, and Erin looked up into the blue-blackness above her. My, but it was glorious! It looked as if God had swirled huge handfuls of fiery diamonds into the darkness, studding the sky with icy light.

"Aren't the stars beautiful tonight?"

Tucker looked up. "They are especially bright . . . 'The heavens declare the glory of God,'" he said quietly, "'and the firmament sheweth His handiwork.'"

"That's from the Bible, isn't it?" Erin asked.

"I believe it's the nineteenth Psalm. Don't look so surprised. You think you and the Preacher are the only folks 'round here that ever read the Good Book?"

"No, of course not, I didn't mean it that way. I just had the impression that you didn't have much use for religion."

Tucker did not reply. He leaned forward and flicked the reins lightly on the horses' backs.

The air was cool, riding in the open wagon. Erin rubbed her hands over the gooseflesh on her arms. Tucker looked down at her.

"You catching a chill?"

"No. I'm fine."

He reached over and touched her hand. "You're cold as spring water." He stopped the horses and removed his suit coat. "Here, put this 'round you."

"I'm fine, really."

"Jist quit bein' stubborn and put it on." He draped the coat over her shoulders and she held it together in front of her.

"Thank you, that does feel better," she said. "It's kind of you to be concerned about me."

Tucker put his foot up on the wagon box and started the horses again. "Ain't nothing," he said. "Anyways, I dasn't have you coming down with the pneumonie; Mattie would skin me alive."

six

Ben rushed through the kitchen, fishing pole in hand, just as Mattie was finishing the breakfast dishes. He grabbed a leftover biscuit from the pan on the stove and stuffed half of it into his mouth. Mattie slapped at his arm.

"Boy, don't you ever git filled up? I declare, it's all I can do to keep you fed these days." She scowled at Ben. "What's that pole in your hand for? You know how I feel about you fishing on Sunday."

Ben put an awkward arm around Mattie's shoulders. "Now, don't be like that, Mattie. Tuck said I could, and there ain't no church today anyway."

"Jist the same, it's the Lord's day," Mattie sniffed. "I reckoned maybe the Preacher would give us a little Bible talk directly."

"Aw, Mattie, he didn't git home from the Pucketts' until after midnight. Like as not he won't even be up by the time I git back. And with the Preacher starting church next week, and then school after that, this might be the last time I can go before winter." Ben grinned. "You know how much you like a sizzling pan of fresh goggle eye."

Mattie appeared to be wavering. "All right, boy. You git along, but make certain you learn me a Scripture verse before dinner time."

"Yes, ma'am!" Ben wasted no time heading out the door.

On impulse, Erin followed him onto the back porch. "Ben?"

"Yes'm?"

"Would you mind if I came along with you?"

"You like to fish, ma'am?"

"To tell the truth, I've never been before in my life, but I'd like to learn. Would you show me how?"

"Surely! I can learn you everything, how to feel when a bass is playing with your bait, how to hook the big ole bucketmouths,

53

and how to head and gut 'em quicker than lightning. Oh—I reckon maybe you ain't quite ready for the guttin' part yet." Ben added quickly, "Don't you fret, I'll clean anything you catch, and maybe you could learn me a short Scripture verse I can say to Mattie when we get back."

"That's a deal. Let me get my bonnet and I'll be ready to go."

The morning air was still cool as they climbed along a bluff downstream of the bridge. Ben spoke quietly as he put their poles down. "See how greenish the water is before us? It don't look it, but that hole is deeper'n our heads. Shallow water's clear through, but the deep holes have color. Look close, there's a big ole grandaddy swimming down near the bottom right now."

At first, Erin couldn't see what Ben was talking about, but then a long gray shadow caught her eye as it slipped silently by in the emerald water.

"Ben, you didn't bring any bait. Don't you need worms or something to get them on the hook?"

"I was figuring to use crawdads. Crawdads and minners are about the best bait there is."

"Really? What are crawdads?"

Ben's eyes widened. "You ain't never seen a crawdad? C'mon down to that low bank over there and I'll show you."

They crunched across the shifting gravel to a place where the river was wide and shallow. Ben squatted down in ankle deep water and carefully turned over a rock. A cloud of sand bubbled up where the rock had been, and when it cleared, a reddish-green miniature lobster appeared.

"That," Ben said. "Is a crawdad." He reached down and snatched the creature up behind its claws, then he put it in a tin pail he had brought from the house.

"Are they hard to catch?"

"No, ma'am, not really. Do y'want to try?"

"Do you think I could?"

"Surely. Let me find a good'n for you." Ben waded over to

the edge of a quiet pool of water. "Here's one you can reach from the bank," he said. "You want to grab him behind those pinchers. If you corner him head on, he'll nip you. Once you start after him, don't stop, or he'll be gone before you git there."

Erin tried again and again, but all she managed to do was to get her shoes wet while the crawdad swam backwards into another hole among the rocks. Finally, she gave up taking aim and slapped her hand down on top of it. Its bony shell writhed between her fingers.

"Got him. . . Ouch!" she cried. She pulled her hand out of the water and saw that a small red welt was swelling on her ring finger. Mr. Crawdad swam back to his rocky home.

"Oh well. Let's hope I can catch fish better than I can catch the bait."

They walked back to the bluff, where Ben baited the hooks and dropped them into the water. He handed Erin a pole. "There," he said. "Now all we got to do is sit back and wait for the fish to bite."

The water sang cheerfully as it flowed over the rocks and wound its way down river. Long-legged insects skated across the water's glossy surface, and in the distance, a cow bell softly clanged.

"You're very lucky to have grown up in a place like this," Erin said. "It's so peaceful and beautiful. Ben, did you ever think how great God must be to create such magnificent country as you have here?"

Ben leaned back on the log and turned his pole around in his hands. "I reckon I ain't thought much about God lately."

"Maybe you should. God loves us so much, Ben."

"If what you say is so, Miz Erin, I think God's got an awful queer way of showing it."

"Things have been hard for you, haven't they? I mean, with your Pa and Ma both gone. I know how much it hurts. I lost my parents when I was young, too."

For just a moment, Ben's eyes reflected pure pain. Then his pole suddenly arched and jerked back and forth until Erin was sure it would snap. Ben patiently worked the fish until it tired, then he lifted it out of the water. Ben said it was a small-mouthed bass, and a good sized one, too. He pushed a thin rope through the gill of the fish and tied the ends to a limb near the river, then he threw the tethered fish back into the water.

"The next one'll be yours, Miz Erin." Ben balanced the end of his pole between his feet and pulled the hook down toward him to put on the fresh bait. He almost had it on when the pole slipped backward in the sand, pulling the hook deep into Ben's thumb.

"Ouch!"

Erin looked the other way while he pulled the hook out. The wound bled freely once it was gone.

"Let me see," she said. "That looks deep."

"Aw, it ain't so much. It is bleeding powerful, though, ain't it?"

"Yes, it is. You probably should wash it out."

Ben dipped his hand into the river, then Erin took a handkerchief from her pocket and bound it around the cut. Once the bandage was in place, the bleeding all but stopped.

"There," Erin said. "Does it still hurt?"

"Just a mite, but it ain't nothing to fret over." Ben looked at the bandage and smiled. "I reckon I'll have me a proud pucker of a scar from this one."

"Yes," Erin agreed. "With any luck, I believe you will. Should we go on back to the house so you can put something on that?"

"No, no need. Besides, I come here to teach you to fish."

For the next hour, they did just that. Erin had to admit that it was exciting to feel an angry fish lurching about on her line, but she was not sure she could ever bring herself to remove a fish from the hook.

"This is fun, Ben. I wish I had tried it years ago."

"You've caught a fine mess. Most women don't like fishin' and such, but you're different."

"Maybe I am, at that. Reverend Teterbaugh will certainly be surprised when we show him what I caught, won't he?"

Ben swirled his feet in the water. "Can I ask you something, Miz Erin?"

"Certainly, Ben, ask away."

"Are you sweet on the Preacher?"

"Sweet? What makes you think that?"

"Just wondering is all."

"I wouldn't exactly say I was 'sweet' on him."

"I don't think I like him much," Ben said. "He's a piddling sort, even for a city feller."

"That's no way to talk. I want you to promise me that you'll give Reverend Teterbaugh a fair chance. All right?"

"All right, Miz Erin, if you say so."

By mid-morning, they had an assortment of bass, goggle eye, and several pretty yellow-bellied fish that Ben called sun perch, all strung up on his rope.

"I expect we best head on back if we want to git these cleaned before dinner time," Ben said. He slung the fish over his shoulder and they walked up toward the bridge. Little frogs bounced across the bank in front of them and plopped into the water.

Erin spotted a huge bullfrog peering up at them out of the plants at the water's edge. She walked right up to it, but the frog remained oddly still.

"Ben, isn't this strange? Why doesn't this big frog hop away like the little ones did?"

She reached down to touch it, but Ben called out, "Hold on, Miz Erin!" and trotted up behind her. He put the fish down on the ground and picked up a tree limb. Cautiously, he prodded at the frog. Then they saw. A large snake, hidden in the shadows of the bridge, was in the process of devouring the bullfrog. The snake thrashed angrily at the touch of Ben's stick.

"C'mon, let's git away from him," Ben said. "That's a moccasin, and I ain't going to disturb him while he's having dinner."

"But can't we do anything? That poor frog."

Ben put the fish back over his shoulder. "The frog's already dead, Miz Erin, but if I had me a rifle gun, I'd fix that old

snake. I reckon I could rock it to death, but Tuck says they
ain't no reason to take chances with snakes if they ain't both-
ering you. Moccasins is the meanest snakes around. Copperheads and rattlers, they'd jist as soon run, most times, than
fool with a man, but moccasins jist natchurly love fighting."

Erin looked back at the snake, trying hard to settle the sick
feeling that had settled in her stomach. "It seems so unfair."

Ben helped her up the embankment to the road. "That's jist
how life is, Miz Erin. You do your best and hope nothing bigger comes along to swaller you up. Ain't no fairness to it a'tall."

Erin wanted to tell Ben that life was not always like that,
that it wasn't all sorrow and cruelty, and God loved him—but
how could she convince a boy who had known so much harsh-
ness?

ح

At dinner, Erin had her first taste of fresh fish dipped in corn-
meal and fried crispy brown. Tucker reached for another helping of buttery hominy and looked her way.

"Ben tells me you're quite a fisherman, Miz Erin," he said.

"Ben did all the hard work," she confessed. "I just held the
pole in between times."

"Tucker," Ben said. "We saw us a big ole moccasin down
under the bridge. Reckon maybe we could git your rifle gun
after dinner and see if we can git him?"

Tucker looked alarmed. "A moccasin? You didn't go messin'
with him, did you?"

"'Course not, Tucker. . ."

"As a matter of fact," Erin said. "Ben kept me from practically putting my hand in that snake's mouth."

Tucker looked at Ben with approval. "It's a lucky thing he
did. Moccasins have a powerful pizen in them. You best hear
this too, Preacher. You always got to keep an eye out for snakes
here. They can be most anywhere, but they especially like holler
logs and rocky ledges. Oft times, you'll find 'em sunning themselves in the middle of the road. Don't never put your hand in
a place you can't see into, and watch real smart where you put

your feet in the woods."

"Could a bite from one of these snakes actually kill someone?" Douglas asked.

"Depends on who got bit and how bad," Tucker said. "Younguns and old folks most often git mortal bites, but a big rattler could kill a grown man, too."

"Not all snakes are bad though," said Ben. "Black snakes eat rats and mice and such. It's a lucky thing to find one in your barn."

"There's also snakes," Jube said, "that do mystifyin' things, like hoop snakes that grab their own tails and roll down the road, or milksnakes that sneak into your barn at night and milk your cows."

Mattie pointedly picked up Jube's plate. "Old man, ain't you got nothing better to do than tell old wives' tales? Why don't you git back to work?"

"Pshaw! Them are facts, jist as sure as the world, and I'm hurt you suspicion me so." Jube's eyes twinkled as he grabbed another chunk of Mattie's gingerbread before he headed out the back door.

Douglas pushed his plate away and leaned back in his chair. "Tucker, with church services starting next Sunday, I'd like to take this week and visit as many families in the area as we can. I was hoping that you might let Ben show us around to the various homes."

Ben brightened. "Could I, Tuck?"

"Ain't you got some chores to do, boy?"

"Yes, sir."

"Then you best git to it, and have Mattie clean up that thumb before you git blood pizened."

Ben got up reluctantly, and went in the kitchen in search of Mattie.

"Fact is, Preacher," said Tucker. "This ain't a good time for Ben to be gone."

"But I thought you had harvested your field crops."

"We have, for a fact, but that don't take account of gitting the grain to the mill, nor the orchard full of apples, nor butchering, not to mention putting up the vegetable garden."

Douglas held up his hand. "All right, you've made your point, but nonetheless, Erin and I must make those visits."

"Most folks live somewheres off the main road, Preacher. I expect you can find all but a few. I'll even set down and draw you up a little map. Then, 'round the end of the week, I reckon we could spare Ben long enough to show you to the back off places."

"I guess that will have to do," Douglas said.

"I reckon it will. Now, if you want Ben to help you later on, I'd be obliged if you'd give us a hand cuttin' firewood. Takes a great pile of wood to see us through the winter. You can handle an ax, can't you?"

"I believe I can. I'll begin as soon as I change my clothes."

seven

Erin picked up another stack of dishes and set them on the shelf. She seemed to spend half her day wiping dishes dry and putting them away; surely a missionary teacher should be doing more important things. Dirty dishes were so unpleasant, with the murky water and floating bits of food. But there was no use whining about it. Anyway, her school would be starting soon.

Mattie threw the dishwater out the back door, then she turned down the damper on the stove and set a pan of beans on the back burner to simmer. "Erin, I got the warshpot about ready t'boil out back. Why don't you gather up all your dirty clothes and we can keep each other company while we scrub."

Laundry! Erin had not even thought of that. At the orphanage, a laundress had been in charge of keeping the children's uniforms clean. Helping in the laundry room was a punishment chore that Erin had quickly learned to avoid. Well, of course she would be expected to do her own laundry here.

"I'll collect everything and be right there, Mattie."

"No need t'hurry, child. Mind, you wear something old."

Fire glowed under the big black kettle set by the creek downstream of the spring house. A raised wooden trough diverted water from the creek to fill the washtubs. A three-legged table made from half a log, flat side up, stood near the kettle. Erin looked around everywhere, but she saw nothing like the washing machines back at the orphanage, not even a washboard.

"Bring them things on down here," Mattie called. "I got everything ready to go. Here's the battling stick." She held out an oar-shaped paddle about a foot long. "Well, child, what ails you?"

"To tell the truth," Erin said, "I have had about as much experience doing laundry as I have had baking pies. I don't know the first thing about washing clothes like this."

Mattie set the battling stick down. "You sure have come to a foreign land, ain't you, child? Well, ain't no trick to warshing clothes. Bring them things over and dump 'em in."

Erin put her clothes in a water-filled tub at the end of the table.

"Git that shirtwaist there and put it on the battling block," Mattie said. "Then, take the stick and wail the tar out of it, like this." She took the battling stick and repeatedly slapped it down hard on the shirtwaist. "This here beats some of the dirt loose out of 'em, then you put it in the kettle to boil for a spell."

"How long will all this take, Mattie? I promised Douglas I would be ready to pay calls with him later this morning."

Mattie took her arm and pulled Erin in front of the battling block. "Won't take long a'tall if you ever git started. You beat these whilst I shave off some soap chips into the kettle."

In a short while, Erin's arms ached and her hands were blistered. By the time she finished the last of her clothes, the battling stick felt as if it weighed fifty pounds. She looked at Mattie with new respect, realizing now the strength required to complete household chores on a farm.

Mattie gave her a reprieve from battling and sent her to stir the clothes with a long wooden paddle. When they were finally clean enough to suit her, Mattie took the paddle, lifted some of the boiling clothes, and put them in the washtub that sat under the waterspout.

"Reckon you can git the rest of these out of the kettle, Erin?" she asked.

Erin scooped the clothes up with the paddle and balancing carefully, started over to the washtub. Unfortunately, she underestimated the weight of the wet clothes and just before she got to the tub, she lost her grip on the handle. The clothes fell on the sandy creek bank.

"Oh, no!" she cried. "Will we have to wash them all over again, Mattie?"

"No, I don't reckon so, that sand'll clean off, but you'll have to rinse 'em extra good."

By the time Erin picked up the clothes and rinsed them, her skirt was splotched with water and sand. She had stooped over to pick up one last stocking when Tucker's voice boomed above her head.

"Miz Erin, is that a new city way of warshin'? We generally don't put clean clothes in the dirt around here."

Erin angrily wheeled around, only to discover that Douglas was with him. Quickly, she tucked up the loose pins in her hair and tried to brush off the sandy dirt which clung to her clothes.

"Don't fancy up on my account, Miz Erin," Tucker said. "I jist come to see if you mind riding horseback on your visits today. The buckboard's needed for hauling grain to the mill. Preacher here says you can ride."

"Yes, I can, if you have a sidesaddle."

Tucker rubbed his chin. "A sidesaddle. I don't know as we have one. . ."

"Tucker, don't you reckon your Ma's old saddle is still up in the loft?" Mattie asked.

"It might be; I'd forgot all about it. I'll go see before I finish loading the wagon." Tucker readjusted his hat and strode off across the yard.

Erin bent over to pick up the washbasket, but it was heavier than she had anticipated. The best she could do was to lift one end and drag it toward the clothesline.

"Hold on," Douglas said. "Let me help you." Erin released the basket, forgetting about the ugly red blisters on her palms. Douglas grasped her wrists.

"Erin, what have you done to your hands?"

"It's from the laundry," she explained. "I'm afraid I'm not used to this kind of work."

"I should think not, and why should you be? You didn't come here to be a housemaid."

"I have to admit, I didn't think about laundry being part of my job, but it's nothing, really."

"I understand that we both have to pull our weight around here," Douglas said. "But I don't think being a missionary should require you to ruin your hands and complexion. After all, a lady is judged by such things in society, and you won't always be working in a backwoods church."

Neither of them realized that Mattie could hear their conversation. She walked over to Douglas, picked up the basket at his feet, and without a word, she went to the clothesline and began hanging up Erin's clothes.

"Douglas, I am afraid we've hurt her feelings."

"I suppose I'd better be more careful of what I say, but she'll be all right, Erin. After all, I only spoke the truth. Why don't we go ahead and start our visits? I'll meet you at the stable as soon as you can freshen up."

Erin didn't feel right about leaving, knowing Mattie had heard them. She walked over and reached into the clothes basket. Mattie pulled a clothespin from her mouth.

"Don't discomfort yourself, Erin," she said. "I can manage."

"Mattie, I'm sorry. I don't mind doing my share, really. Everything is just so new to me, that's all."

Mattie finished pinning the skirt to the line, then she turned toward Erin and smiled. "I know, child; it's all right." She took a pair of drawers from the basket and resumed her work. "Erin, the Lord has put you heavy on my heart," she said. "Your young head is so full of dreams and such. But you got to decide which dreams are from the Lord and which dreams are jist Erin's. I'll tell you a secret, child. You generally have to do some bone-tiring work to make the Lord's dreams come true, and even then your own strength ain't near enough. I jist want you to find God's best."

"I'm ready to work, Mattie, truly I am, and I won't complain again. I do want God to use me here at Lost Creek."

Mattie put her gnarled hand on Erin's. "'Seek ye first the Kingdom,' child, and don't settle for nothin' less."

❧

Erin quickly changed clothes and packed a lunch (or dinner, as they called it here) in a flour sack. She hoped she had not lost Mattie's respect with her hasty words. Somehow, what

Mattie thought of her mattered very much.

Douglas was waiting for her in the pasture with a handsome buckskin gelding and a chestnut mare. He helped Erin onto the mare, and then he mounted. He reached down and patted his horse's neck.

"He's a beauty, isn't he?" Erin said.

They left the pasture and started down the road at a fast trot, then crossed the bridge and went on through the woods to where the road flattened out and followed a dry creek bed.

"I don't suppose you would be interested in a little race, would you?" Erin asked. "Say down to that fork in the road?"

Douglas pulled up his horse. "A race? Does the lady wish to make a wager?"

"I didn't think ministers were allowed to do that. All right, the loser washes the schoolhouse windows."

"Fair enough, ma'am. Anytime you are ready."

Erin kicked her horse into a full gallop. The horses' hooves pounded loudly on the gravel, and the rocking rhythm of the powerful horse beneath her made Erin want to go faster and faster as the dust and rocks flew up around them. They stayed neck and neck until the end, but just before the finish, Erin's horse pulled forward and beat Douglas' by a nose.

"I bow to the champion!" Douglas shouted, and he bent dramatically from the waist. They both were laughing so hard that they didn't notice the wagon until it was a few feet away.

"Well, how do, Preacher, Miz Erin," called Silas Butler. "I heard you all the way acrosst the crick. . . From all the carrying on, I thought that there might be some trouble. Bless the Lord, you're all right."

"I'm sorry, Reverend Butler," Erin said. "I am afraid we were awfully noisy."

"Time was when people might take your cutting didoes like that the wrong way, you being out here alone and all, but I reckon most folks would make allowances."

"What brings you out on the road today?" Douglas asked.

"Oh, a widder woman from Grassy Holler's been poorly for

some time now and she up and died night before last. The family sent for me to do the funeralizin'. We had us a fine shouting service to send her on. People come from miles around with enough food to feed Grant's army. You two jist out for a frolic?"

"No," Erin answered quickly. "We're on our way to the Kellers'. We intend to visit everyone we possibly can before we start church services next Sunday."

"Still head set on starting next week are you? Well, Preacher, I'd be obliged if you'd spread around about the protracted meetings as you visit."

"I will try to remember, Reverend Butler."

"Miz Corbett, I reckon I can save you a trip out to my place if you can tell me the particulars of when to start my younguns in your school."

"We are hoping to start in two weeks. I could let you know for certain at the brush arbor meetings."

"That'd be fine." Reverend Butler wiped his face on a crumpled red handkerchief. "Well, the Lord bless you in your travels." He turned his horse and bounced the wagon up the hill.

"The old windbag."

"Hush, Douglas. He'll hear you."

"I'm sorry, but every time he sees me he makes it a point to put me in my place."

"Think how he must feel with your taking over one of his churches," Erin said. "He probably doesn't mean to be rude. We're just not accustomed to these hill people's bluntness."

"Maybe so, Erin, but that man irritates me." Douglas pulled his horse's head up from the grass it had been eating. "If we want to make more than one visit today, we had better get going."

The Kellers were one family Erin was looking forward to visiting, since she had already met them on the night of the pie supper. Their house was much smaller than the Gillams' place. It looked like two little houses connected together by a covered passageway called a dog-run.

Erin and Douglas no more than got into the yard before little Beth and Walter and an assortment of hound dogs came running to meet them. Walter ushered them into the front door, while Beth went to the kitchen to fetch her mother. Mrs. Keller came out with a juicy blackberry pie and set it down on the table.

"Preacher, Miz Erin," she said. "It's so nice to see you again. We're proud to have you at our house. Come set and have a piece of pie. It's still warm." Mrs. Keller was already setting plates on the table.

"I'm jist silly about blackberries," she said, "Every year we dry all the children and me can pick."

"Mrs. Keller, this is about the best pie I've ever tasted in my life," Douglas said. "If you bring these along to the dinners on the ground each Sunday, I'm afraid I won't be able to concentrate on my sermons."

"Preacher, how you talk. Asa and me are happy as can be about having us an every-Sunday church, and a school to boot. I been wishing for the children to take up books for quite a spell now. You jist let us know what can we do to help. Asa's a fine hand at making things, and I'd be proud to run up some curtains for the schoolhouse if you've a mind."

"Why, that would be lovely," Erin said. "Thank you."

The next home was the Witbecks'. The Witbeck cabin was made of hand-notched logs which had worn to a silvery gray, and the roof was covered with split wood shingles. A stone chimney stood on one end of the cabin, and Erin assumed the lean-to on the other end was the kitchen. The only light the cabin received was from one small window and the front door, which stood open. Douglas and Erin dismounted and walked to the edge of the yard.

"I don't see any dogs," Douglas said.

"Just the same, I think we should call out like Jube told us to."

Douglas shrugged and cupped his hands to his mouth. "Hello? Is anyone there?" Immediately, two skinny mongrels raced down the hill behind the cabin and came straight toward them. Douglas and Erin froze.

"Hello?" Erin called. "Mrs. Witbeck?"

The dogs were almost to the garden fence, when Mrs. Witbeck came out from behind a shed in the back yard. "Deke! Blackie! Git your worthless hides out of here. Go on, git!" The dogs slunk away to the other side of the cabin.

Douglas stepped forward and offered his hand. "Good morning, Mrs. Witbeck."

The woman's face brightened. "Preacher, how do! Don't mind them fool dogs, they got a lot of noise is all. What brings you and the teacher up here today? Come in and set."

The interior of the cabin was dark and cool and smelled of wood smoke.

"There's settin' chairs over yonder. Would you like some coffee?"

"No, thank you," Douglas said. "I'm afraid Mrs. Keller filled us up with pie and cider a little while ago. We just stopped by to invite your family to the first church service Sunday morning."

"And to see how many of your children will be coming to our school," Erin added.

"John and me's got three younguns, all tickled to death about the new school. Our oldest one's Will, he's ten, then there's Jackson, who's eight, and our leastun is Annie, she's six. They all went nut hunting with their daddy. I expect they'll be back right soon now. My twenty-sixth birthin' day is tomorrow and I been wishing for some black walnuts to make a cake, so John up and took off this morning to fetch me some."

"Many happy returns, Mrs. Witbeck," Douglas said. "I hope we will see you all at church Sunday."

"I reckon jist about everybody'll come to hear the new city preacher, don't you fret none about that."

John Witbeck and his children returned with a tow sack filled with greenish-black balls. Will took a ball from the sack and proudly cut it open, revealing the hard black walnut inside, while Annie sidled up to Erin and fingered the lace around her wrists.

"Are you stayin' for dinner?" Annie asked.

"We'd be proud to have you," said Mrs. Witbeck.

"That's very kind," Douglas said. "But we really should be going."

"You jist got here," Mrs. Witbeck said. "'Sides, we got more'n enough, and you got to eat somewhere."

The Witbecks insisted despite their protests, and soon everyone was feasting on a combination of Erin's picnic food and Mrs. Witbeck's dinner. It was a pleasant meal, but Erin couldn't help feeling sorry that she and Douglas would not be having their quiet picnic together. Erin didn't want to admit it, even to herself, but keeping her mind off Douglas and on the mission work was becoming more and more difficult.

❧

Douglas and Erin rode out each morning for the next three days and made as many calls as they could before the sun set. As the week progressed, Erin began to understand why Jube had described the Gillam home as "a glory of a house." By Lost Creek standards, Tucker was wealthy indeed.

Most of their congregation lived in tiny log cabins with only one or two rooms. The homes were dark and crowded with no indoor plumbing. Brothers and sisters thought nothing of sleeping three or more to a bed. Many families walked a quarter of a mile to the nearest spring every time they needed fresh water.

Window glass was a luxury enjoyed by only three families. Most windows were covered with oiled paper or simply left open during the summer months and boarded up in the winter. In warm weather, all manner of flying "gallynippers" buzzed in the cabins at will. Leftover food had to be covered immediately with a cloth to keep away the flies.

Yet these people did not seem to consider themselves poor. The men they met were fiercely proud of their land and their families and in performing a good day's work. They were solid, practical people who seemed satisfied with their lot in life, much more satisfied, Erin realized, than most of the people she knew back home, who were incredibly rich by comparison.

Ben joined them on Saturday, as Tucker had promised. The last visits were in homes that were accessible only by footpath, and without Ben they would have been impossible to find. These deep woods cabins were the poorest of all.

The last visit they planned to make was to the Hinkles'. It took an hour of hard walking before Ben finally stopped and pointed to a cabin jutting out of the side of a hill.

"There it is," he said. "I best go first. Mr. Hinkle might take it in his mind to get ornery if he sees a stranger coming on his place."

The cabin leaned precariously on a piled rock foundation. Old rags had been stuffed here and there among the logs where the chinking had long since washed out. A spindly stand of corn grew in an uptilted field behind the cabin. Even the fragrant scent from the pine trees could not camouflage the smell of pigs and dogs and, apparently, people who used the yard for an outhouse.

"Mr. Hinkle? It's Ben Gillam. We come to see you."

A shadowy figure appeared in the doorway, then Mr. Hinkle stepped out into the yard. He was a thin man, dressed in a dirty union suit and ragged overalls.

"Howdy, Mr. Hinkle," Ben said. "I brung the new preacher and school teacher t'meet you."

Mr. Hinkle squinted at them through cold eyes. "What they want to come up here for?"

Douglas stepped forward and offered his hand. "How do you do, Mr. Hinkle. We've been visiting everyone to tell them that church services will begin tomorrow." After a moment, Douglas lowered his hand and put it in his pocket.

"We're also starting a school," Erin said. "I was wondering how many of your children might be old enough to attend."

"Well now, lady, jist what makes y'think I want my younguns going to any school of yours?"

There was a rustling sound from just inside the cabin door.

"Seth, could I speak to you?" said a timid voice.

"Git in the house, Narcissy. You ain't fit to be seen."

Something in Mr. Hinkle's tone of voice irked Erin. She walked past him to the door of the cabin. "Mrs. Hinkle? I am Erin Corbett, the mission school teacher."

Mrs. Hinkle stepped into the doorway and nodded, then turned frightened eyes to her husband. "Seth, I'd be pleasured if the younguns could git some book learnin'," she said.

"I said to git in the house, woman."

Mrs. Hinkle stepped back from the door. She was obviously in a family way, and due fairly soon from the look of it. A chubby little boy peeked shyly from around her skirts.

"Perhaps we could visit sometime when it is more convenient for you," Erin said. Mrs. Hinkle nodded again and disappeared into the darkness of the cabin. Erin turned back to Mr. Hinkle.

"I would very much like to have your children in our school. I hope you will consider sending them."

Mr. Hinkle did not look at her when he spoke. "Only got three younguns growed up to any size," he said. "The little'n, my boy Rabe, and Sariah. Got another three buried yonder on the hill. Took milksick when they was babies."

"I'm sorry," Erin said.

Mr. Hinkle looked blankly at her, then he continued. "Might let the girl go, she's too piddling to help much around here anyway. Might git her out from underfoot till the new one comes."

"That would be fine," Erin said. "I hope you'll think about sending your son, too."

"Don't know as I want no lady teacher telling my boy what to do. I'll study on it."

Mr. Hinkle picked up an ax that leaned against the cabin wall and walked abruptly off to a scattered woodpile down the hill.

They started back home, plodding down the steep path that led away from the cabin. Erin slapped at the tree branches in her way, forgetting that Douglas was behind her.

"Watch out!" Douglas cried. "Are you trying to decapitate me?"

"I'm sorry, Douglas, but when I think of Mr. Hinkle, I get angry all over again."

"If it is any consolation, I don't think Mr. Hinkle was too impressed with you either."

"Mr. Hinkle don't like no woman standing up t'him like you did," Ben said.

"Perhaps I shouldn't have done it, but I felt so sorry for his poor wife. From the look of that filthy place, Mr. Hinkle doesn't waste much time taking care of his family."

"The Hinkles have always had a bad case of swamp measles, that's for certain," Ben said.

"Swamp measles? What is that?" Douglas asked.

"Oh, I reckon you'd jist call it being dirty. It ain't easy keeping a family clean what with the spring being off such a far piece from the house."

"Then why doesn't he build closer to water?" Erin asked. "It doesn't seem like that land he's on could possibly produce enough to support a family."

"Mr. Hinkle likes to keep to hisself," said Ben. "He ain't first off a farmer, anyway. Most cash money he makes is from selling nuts and sang root and wild honey and such to the Berryman store. And I reckon he does all right with his corn."

"He really grows enough from that sickly crop to make money?" Douglas asked.

"Not as it comes off of the stalk," Ben said. "But by the time he bottles it and packs it down the mountain, it's worth a considerable sum."

"You're talking about moonshining then," Douglas said.

"Liquor?" Erin said indignantly. "You know he makes corn liquor and no one does anything about it? Why not?"

Ben turned and held out his hand to help Erin over a large log which had fallen across the path. "Well, ma'am, most folks around here think that what a man does on his own property is his own business. People who say otherwise have been known to git theirselves hurt."

eight

The next Sunday they pulled into a schoolyard filled with wagons. Even Tucker had consented to attend in honor of Douglas' first sermon. He helped Mattie and Erin out of the wagon while Jube tethered the horses.

People were packed inside the school room. Children filled the small seats in the front, and the older girls and women sat in the larger desks toward the back. The men and boys stood along the walls or found places just outside, near an open window. The Reynolds were there, and the Kellers, and the Witbecks. Bessie Puckett and her mother sat in prominent seats near the front. Mattie and Erin found seats just as Douglas strode up to the small pulpit that had been put on the platform in place of Erin's desk.

"Good morning," he said. "I am delighted to see such a grand crowd assembled to worship here today. Let us begin with prayer. Shall we bow our heads?"

Erin couldn't seem to keep her mind on what Douglas was saying. He was so handsome in his trim black suit, and his voice had a resonant quality when he was behind the pulpit. He seemed like an entirely different person. Erin could think of nothing she wanted more than to be a part of a ministry such as his. Perhaps their being assigned there together was more than just a coincidence.

Douglas had just begun to speak in earnest when Erin noticed some sort of disruption in the back corner of the room. Men looked at one another and shifted uncomfortably. The ladies near them fidgeted and began to fan themselves. Then Erin smelled it too, the unmistakable odor of skunk. It seemed to be coming up from the floorboards. Douglas gamely continued preaching, not knowing why he had lost the congregation's attention, until finally the scent pervaded the entire room.

Isaac Reynolds wrinkled his nose. "Ooh-we!" he cried out

loud. "Don't that polecat stink! He must be right under the floor."

A hasty evacuation followed. Douglas brought up the rear, holding his handkerchief over his nose. Several of the men began removing boards from around the foundation to provide the skunk a route of escape. The children laughed and ran about, while the adults stood in small groups commenting on what a shame it was that a varmint had spoiled church on the Preacher's first day.

Erin was going to ask Douglas what she should do about Sunday School when she noticed that he was staring off toward the road. Amid the flurry of activity, Silas Butler stood quietly by his wagon, his arms crossed over his chest. Enlo sat on the wagon seat, holding the reins, with the same sarcastic smirk on his face that he had the night of the pie supper. Douglas made his way to them through the crowd.

"Having a little trouble, are you, Brother?" Reverend Butler asked.

"Yes, it seems a skunk found his way under the building just as I began my sermon. Isn't that rather odd? I have read that skunks are mostly nocturnal animals, yet this one chooses to visit a noisy building full of people right in the middle of the day."

"Well, Brother, you jist never know about critters. I've seen them do some peculiar things in my time."

"I imagine you have," Douglas said. "What brings you here today? I thought you would be preaching somewhere."

"No, I ain't found a new church to take the place of this here one yet. Besides, with the protracted meetings starting tomorrow, I can't hardly travel too far off. Enlo and I been visiting some folks who don't go to church regular, and givin' them an invite to the meetings. We were jist on our way now to set up the brush arbor." Butler looked across the yard. "It won't discomfort you none if I ask some of the men to help me, will it, being that you've kindly give up on the services and all . . . ?"

Douglas' cheeks burned. "By all means, go ahead," he said.

"Thank you, Brother, and you surely are welcome to come to the meetings, too. We're gonna have some real preaching there."

Douglas' eyes flashed fire. "Now look here. . ."

"Reverend Butler?" Erin said. "I just wanted to let you know that our school will start a week from tomorrow. Lessons begin at nine o'clock."

"Why thank you, Miz Corbett. My younguns'll be there for certain."

Families brought out their dinners and ate in the shade, and then many of the men went to help Reverend Butler build the brush arbor. Before Jube left, he made a quick trip inside the schoolhouse to rescue Erin's *Kind Words* booklets so that they could at least have Sunday School for the children.

As soon as everyone finished dinner, Erin sat the children in a circle under the giant oak in the schoolyard and fumbled her way through her first lesson. The children squirmed, and Erin stammered, but somehow they got through it. By the time everyone began to leave, Erin was worn out.

Only four people rode back in the wagon to the farmhouse. Jube had left to help Reverend Butler, and Ben was walking home with some of his friends. Tucker turned the wagon around and started the horses down the long hill home.

"Preacher," Tucker said, "I'll say one good thing for your sermon today—it was short."

Douglas was in no mood to joke about the day's service. "I suppose short sermons please you, Tucker," he said.

"They got their advantages. After that polecat came on out, we nailed the boards up again on the backside of the schoolhouse. I don't reckon you'll be troubled by any more varmints."

"I don't imagine we'd have quite that same problem ever again anyway," Douglas said. "Whoever did it would be too smart for that."

"You saying that skunk had some help gitting under the schoolhouse?" Tucker asked.

"Now who'd go and do such a thing?" Mattie said. "We ain't the kind of folks to do foolery on the Lord's day."

"The Preacher might be right, Mattie. I found a gunny sack back of the schoolhouse that smelled something awful of skunk."

"If that is someone's idea of a joke," Erin said, "I don't think it's very funny."

The horses had just stopped in front of the house when Jube came loping toward them.

"What's wrong, Jube?" Tucker asked.

"We lost another cow, and this time they butchered her right spang on our land."

"Where?"

"Back in the woods between here and the river. I was looking for some saplings to cut for the brush arbor and I come acrosst it, not thirty feet from the road."

"Did you find any tracks?"

"No, you could see where the grass had been trampled, but there wasn't a trail anywhere off in the woods. They must have toted the meat to the road and carted it off in a buckboard. It was a fresh kill, last day or so."

"I better go take a look," Tucker said.

❧

Mattie was as excited as a child at Christmas all day Monday. She hurried everyone through the morning chores, and as soon as dinner was done, she put all the leftovers in a stewpot and banked the fire in the stove.

"That ought to keep it for a spell," she said. "The water's hot in the reservoir, let's us have a bath before the meeting tonight."

The tin bathtub was dragged into Mattie's room, since it was closest to the kitchen, and Erin undressed and sat down. Mattie poured a bucket of warm water over her shoulders while Erin scrubbed.

"Are these meetings very different from regular church services?" Erin asked.

"Well, child, that depends on what you're used to. When I was a girl we had protracted meetings that'd last two weeks or more. People'd come from miles around and camp out right on the grounds. The men would make coverings of holiness, as they called them, to seat upwards of two hundred folks. The best meetings had at least three preachers. They'd start in at the morning and preach again in the afternoon, and then they'd have the big meeting with testimony times and prayer at night. Folks would sing and pray—and, Erin, sometimes you'd feel as if the hand of God jist reached down and touched that place. Those were precious days."

Erin stepped out of the tub and Mattie handed her a towel.

"This meeting won't be nearly as big," Mattie said. "Of course, size don't matter none to the Master. He's joyous to find jist one heart ready to let Him be Lord."

Mattie set out a quick supper that night, so that they could be on their way just as soon as the dishes were done. As Erin spread the dish towels to dry, Mattie picked up her bonnet and went to the stairwell. "Ben, you git a move on," she called.

Ben clomped downstairs looking uncomfortable and dejected in his Sunday suit. "It don't feel natural gitting dressed up on a Monday," he said. "This collar pinches my neck."

Mattie was not in a sympathetic mood. "You stop that whining and go fetch me an old quilt from the chest in the attic. I don't want to set on splinters all night. Mind you hurry, now."

"Yes'm."

"I best go see if that Jube has got hisself ready to go," Mattie said. "Like as not he's laying around that cabin gathering wool."

Tucker looked up from his book. "Mattie, why don't you stop flying 'round this room? Jube left for the meeting half an hour ago with some spare lanterns."

"Oh. . .well, I reckon we're ready then." Mattie pulled her shawl up around her shoulders. "Tucker, it wouldn't do you no harm if you were to come along."

"Not tonight, thank you. I'm gonna spend the evening with Mr. Dickens here."

Mattie sighed. "Well, do as you think best. Ben, you come on."

There was no need for a lantern as they walked to the meeting; a giant harvest moon lit their path with its warm light. Douglas took Erin's arm as they walked through the shadows.

"Mattie is certainly looking forward to these meetings," Erin said.

"Yes, but I'm not sure I share her enthusiasm. The moonlight is beautiful tonight, isn't it?"

"Yes, it is. I believe these meetings will be interesting. They'll give us a chance to meet people and to see what kind of worship services they're used to."

"I suppose," Douglas said. "Have I seen that hat before? It's very becoming."

"No, this is the first time I've worn it, thank you. I wonder why Tucker didn't come? Mattie said everyone comes to these protracted meetings. Sometimes I wonder why Tucker bothered to board us and help set up the mission. He doesn't seem to care much about the church. Have you noticed?"

"I've noticed he doesn't care much for me."

"I don't think he likes me much better. He can be so aggravating. But did you see what he was reading tonight? Imagine, a man like Tucker Gillam reading *David Copperfield*."

"Quite honestly," Douglas said, "I haven't given Tucker Gillam that much thought."

Up ahead, the arbor sat in a clearing on a wide gravel bank near the river. It reminded Erin of the jungle huts she had seen in picture books as a child. Young pine trees had been used for the support poles which held up a tree limb roof. Beneath the arbor, there were rows of split-log pews, and sawdust had been spread thickly on the ground. Lanterns hung on the posts and a special platform had been erected up front for the preacher to stand on. Mattie waved them over to where she had spread her quilt on a pew, and they took their seats.

The crowd hushed as Reverend Butler stepped up on the platform. He raised his hand and smiled broadly. "Good evening, folks."

The crowd responded politely, but Reverend Butler was not

satisfied. "I said, good evening!"

This time the congregation gave a loud "good evening" back to Reverend Butler. He seemed satisfied and continued, "Ain't God give us a glorious night? If you think so, say 'Amen!'"

Loud "amens" sounded from every corner of the arbor.

"Bless the Lord, I'm proud to see such a goodly crowd come out tonight." Reverend Butler looked directly at Erin. "I thought to start off the testifying, maybe our new teacher would favor us with a word."

Pure panic overtook Erin. What could she possibly say in front of all these people? She dared not decline; after all, missionaries were supposed to be ready to speak "in season and out."

"Stand right on up, Miz Erin, so's we can all hear," said Reverend Butler.

She got to her feet, searching frantically for the right words to say. She was keenly aware of all the eyes that were now focused directly on her.

"Well, uh, I suppose. . .that is, I'm not sure where to begin. You see. . .I have, um, been a Christian most of my life. I asked Christ into my heart when I was a little girl." She wiped her sweaty palms on her skirt. "And when I heard a sermon about being a missionary to the poor people of Missouri—oh, not that I think the people here are poor—that's just what the evangelist said in his sermon." She was making a mess of this. "Anyway, here I am. Oh, and I hope, uh, that if you aren't a Christian, you will become one. Thank you."

When she sat down, Erin's heart was pounding in her throat. *That was perfectly dreadful,* she thought. *I practically called them all indigent bumpkins.* When they stood to sing a song before the offering, Erin slipped quietly away into the darkness.

Once she had made her escape, she stopped for a moment and watched through the trees. Reverend Butler was holding up a worn black Bible. "Bless the Lord," he said. "Tonight I'll tell you about the wheat and the tares. Hallelujah! I'm preaching out of the gospel of Matthew."

Reverend Butler read haltingly from the Scripture, mispronouncing several of the words. His face glistened and his shirt clung to his back as he paced to and fro on the platform, pounding the podium and gesturing wildly.

"Are you wheat or a weed?" he shouted. "Wheat or a weed? Wheat or weed?"

Erin turned and walked down the road. In the distance, the whippoorwills were calling. "Wheat or weed?" they seemed to say, "Wheat or weed?" She had thought all the right words would be ready, but they had not come. It wasn't just nerves, or being new at her job; something deep down wasn't right. "Wheat or weed?" She felt awfully weed-like tonight.

When she reached the edge of the yard she did not go in the house, for fear that Tucker would still be in the parlor. Instead, she walked around back and sat down on a stump by the little stream. In the distance, the hills stood out black against the night sky. The stream made soft gurgling sounds at her feet.

What was it that troubled her so? She sat in the quiet of the yard, trying to understand why she felt so incompetent. . .so powerless. Then, from the valley below, Erin heard the distant voices of the congregation singing the invitation hymn.

"Cast thy burden on the Lord," came the words, rising faintly through the trees. "Lean thou only on His Word; Ever will He be thy stay, Tho' the heav'ns shall melt away."

"Dear Lord," she prayed. "This is so much harder than I thought it would be. Please help me. Please do whatever it takes to make me the kind of missionary You want me to be."

She must have lost track of the time, for as she went back toward the house at last, Douglas and Tucker came out of the back door with lanterns.

"Erin, where have you been?" Douglas asked. "I looked everywhere for you after the service."

Tucker grinned. "I thought maybe you was et by a wampus kitty."

"I'm sorry. I went for a little walk. I didn't realize I had been gone so long."

They all went back into the kitchen, and Tucker blew out the lanterns. Douglas waited until Tucker had climbed the stairs.

"Erin, please don't ever run off like that again," he said. "I was terribly worried."

"I really am sorry, Douglas. I felt so stupid after giving my testimony tonight. I just had to get away."

"There was nothing wrong with what you said, and it was very unfair of Butler to embarrass you like that."

"No, I should have been able to speak. I am a missionary, after all."

"A very new missionary, who is allowed to make mistakes the first time she speaks publicly. You're just tired, Erin." Douglas slipped his hand over hers. "Get some rest." His lips brushed her forehead before he went out the door toward his cabin.

nine

The sun had just begun to glisten through the trees when Erin started on her way to the school house. She had spent the entire week before school with her teaching books, preparing lesson plans. She planned to pattern her school after the great educator J. H. Pestalozzi. Erin had read Pestalozzi's philosophies in a book one of her teachers had loaned her, and his ideas fascinated her. Erin vowed her students would receive the most modern education possible, regardless of their modest facilities.

The school house was freshly scrubbed and ready for the children. *McGuffy Reader*s were stacked neatly on Erin's desk next to the *Ray's Arithmetic*s and the *Blue-backed Speller*s. Mattie had confided to Erin that Tucker had ordered the textbooks, enough for one set of books per family.

Erin checked the ink and quills and set out the Bible that the mission board had supplied. Finally, she walked down the hill to the well and drew a bucket of drinking water. That was a job, she decided, that would soon belong to one of the boys with stronger arms than hers.

A half dozen pupils were already clustered in the schoolyard though it was not yet eight-thirty. Beth Keller was there with her tow-headed brothers, Walter and Noah. Erin recognized some of the Reynolds children, too, rolling in the dirt a few feet from the door of the schoolhouse. A broad-shouldered lad pulled them to their feet by the scruffs of their necks. *That must be the oldest Reynolds boy,* thought Erin.

Erin took the bell from her desk and went to the door. "Come in, children. . .come in quietly and put your dinner pails on the shelf, then we will go about getting your seats."

Erin asked everyone to line up by her desk. Beginning with the Reynolds children, she carefully printed their names in her roll book.

"All right, you are Isaac Reynolds. And how old are you, Isaac?"

Isaac gave her a toothless grin. "I'm seven, ma'am."

"Fine. And you are Joshua." Joshua nodded solemnly. Erin turned to the oldest boy. "I'm sorry, I don't know your name."

"My name's Ameriky Reynolds, and I was fourteen years old last fourth of July—that's why my Daddy named me like he did—after our country."

"That is very patriotic," Erin said. "Ameriky, do you and your brothers know how to read?"

"Oh yes'm. Ma's been teaching us at home every bit she can. Even Isaac can pick out some words now and again, when he ain't being ornery." Isaac wrinkled a freckled nose and stuck his tongue out at his brother.

"That will do, Isaac," Erin said.

"My daddy said to tell you t'whup the fool out'n us if we give you any bother," Ameriky said.

"I don't think that will be necessary. You older boys sit near the back for now, and Isaac, you find yourself a seat on the boys' side near the front."

"Yes'm," said Isaac. "And Teacher?"

"What, Isaac?"

Isaac leaned toward Erin and whispered, "I think you're real pretty." He turned and trotted to his seat.

For the next hour, Erin interviewed a steady stream of children. At the end of the line, to Erin's surprise, were Rabe and Sariah Hinkle. Rabe seemed much like his father, with a bitter and hopeless air about him, though he was only eleven. Sariah was a pleasant surprise, though, for she crept up close to Erin's desk and smiled.

"Teacher, my name's Sariah and I brung ya these daisies from along the way to be a beauty on your desk."

"Thank you, Sariah," Erin said. "They're lovely."

She looked up then to see Enlo lumber in with a frail, dark-haired girl trailing behind him. He pushed the girl to the side and gave Erin a sullen look.

"Enlo, is this your sister?" Erin asked.

"Well, she sure ain't my sweetheart."

The children laughed at his joke, and Enlo smiled, obviously pleased to find an audience.

"Come here, Enlo," Erin said firmly. Enlo looked back at the children and sauntered over to her desk.

"Enlo, I think it would be nice if we spoke in respectful tones to one another. So, let's start again. I need to put your name and age in my roll book. How old are you?"

"Reckon I'm 'bout nineteen. Don't nobody know my birthin' date for certain."

"I see, and your sister. . ." Erin looked up and saw that the girl was still standing by the door. "Come here, dear, and tell me your name."

She crept up to the desk. "My name is Winifred, ma'am," she whispered. "I'm thirteen."

She was small for her age and rather homely, with an abnormality around her mouth—not a hare-lip exactly, perhaps a scar—that caused her to speak with a lisp.

"Enlo, you take a seat in the back row, and Winifred, perhaps you would like to sit next to Lela."

Enlo moved toward his desk, again shoving Winifred out of the way. "Move, snot nose," he snarled.

"Enlo! We will not tolerate name calling in this class," Erin said.

"I'm terrible sorry, Teacher," said Enlo, grinning. He slumped down into a back row seat.

They spent the rest of the morning passing out books, and then Erin had each child read from the *McGuffey's* and do some simple arithmetic. Of seventeen children, only eight could read, and a few more than that could "cipher." Erin decided it might be best to start most of them in the primer and allow them to progress at their own speed.

ta

As the first weeks went by, Erin encountered problems she had not anticipated.

The children's clothes were worn thin and yellowed from

repeated washings in river water, and most of them wore no shoes. Though the children seemed to pay the weather no heed, Erin hesitated to send them outside to play with so little protection from the chilly autumn wind.

Her biggest problem, however, was classroom discipline. The titters and giggles at Enlo on the first day had been replaced by outright laughter, horseplay, and practical jokes. Twice, Erin had retrieved sweet gum burrs from her chair just before she'd sat down on them, and all manner of vermin and reptiles had been placed in her desk drawers. She was sure that Enlo was behind most of this foolery, but she could never catch him in the act. Pestalozzi's philosophies did not seem to be working very well in Erin's classroom.

"May I have your attention, class?" Erin said one day. "Remember that we will have our weekly spelling bee Friday afternoon using this week's lesson in your *Blue-back*."

Out of the corner of her eye, Erin saw Enlo poke Rabe Hinkle in the ribs. Enlo said something and they both went into convulsions of laughter.

"Enlo, do you want to share your joke with the class?" Erin asked.

"Naw, I reckon this bunch of clod-kickers jist wouldn't understand what we was talking about."

"Then please be quiet."

Enlo shifted in his chair. "No city woman teacher is gonna tell me when to shut my mouth. If I want to talk, I'll talk."

The silence was uncomfortable as teacher and pupil glared at each other, neither backing down. Erin did not know what to do next, but Ben made the decision for her. He stood up by his desk.

"Teacher said to hush your mouth, Enlo."

Enlo heaved himself to his feet and turned toward Ben.

"Class," Erin said nervously. "I think we're all a little tired. We'll dismiss a few minutes early today."

Enlo gave Ben a withering look and skulked out of the door with Rabe close at his heels. The rest of the children filed out while Erin gathered up her papers. She sat down in her chair and closed her eyes, but her rest was short-lived. Angry voices sounded out in the school yard.

"Teacher's pet!" Enlo taunted. "Ain't you jist the sweetest thing."

Erin hurried to the door. Ben had set his books on the ground and stood square in front of Enlo.

"You best move out of my way, Butler," Ben said.

"You think you're such a much, telling me to shut up, Mr. High-and-Mighty Gillam. Maybe I ought to thump you on the head a little, then you might think twice before you try to take up for the Teacher."

"Enlo," Ben said, "unless you want to git your ears pinned back beside your head, you best turn your shiftless self towards home."

"You ain't near big enough for that kind of talk, little Ben. Must be real nice having the Teacher at your place. She tuck you in at night and kiss you on the ear?"

Ben flew into Enlo with both fists flailing. Erin ran out into the yard and shouted for them to stop, but the boys ignored her. They were both stronger than she, so there was nothing Erin could do to make them quit.

To Erin's relief, Jube came running across the yard and wedged himself between the boys. The rest of the children scattered as Jube struggled to keep them apart. Enlo lunged at Ben, but Jube caught him with an open-handed cuff that sent him reeling backward.

"That's enough!" Jube shouted.

Enlo sat up and put his hand to his face. "Old man, you like to broke my jaw."

"When I like to, boy, I will. Now, git yourself on home."

"Enlo," Erin said, "I think your father and I should have a talk before you return to school."

Enlo straightened himself slowly and took a few steps. Before he continued on, he turned and spat on the ground at Ben's feet. Ben tried to pull away from Jube, but Jube had a firm grip on his arm.

"Hold on now," Jube said. "Jist settle down. Are you all right, boy?"

"Yes, sir, I reckon so." Ben wiped away the blood that trickled from his nose.

"Well, you better have a purty stout reason for fighting at school by the time you git to the house, or Tucker may jist finish off what Enlo started. You git on down the road and have Mattie fix you up."

Ben picked up his books and turned to go.

"Ben?"

"Yes, ma'am?"

"Thank you for standing up for me in class. I'm sorry it got you into a fight with Enlo. I'll explain things to Tucker, if it will help."

"No'm. I reckon if you can't take Enlo on, you sure ain't no match for Tucker."

Ben disappeared around the curve in the road, but his words still pricked at Erin's heart.

"You been having trouble at the school, Miz Erin?" Jube asked.

"Oh, a few students have been somewhat difficult, but I think in time we can all be friends."

"Well, what the world, if those ya-hoos don't straighten up, you jist tell ole Jube. I'll come clean their plows for you."

"Thank you, Jube, but I'm afraid this is one problem I have to solve on my own. I just wish I knew where to start."

☙

The next morning brought a cold wind and low, gray clouds. The children arrived and formed a circle around the stove, warming icy fingers and toes. Already the cold had brought on sniffling noses. As they warmed themselves, the room began to buzz with their voices.

"Have y'heard, Teacher?" Ameriky asked. "There's gonna be a barn raising next Saturday for Emmit and Rose Stiles."

"A barn raising?" Erin asked. "What's that?"

The children stared at her in disbelief. "Ain't you never been to a raising?" asked Noah Keller.

"I'm afraid not. Perhaps you could explain it to me."

"Well," Noah said, "It's the way folks help a family put up a new barn. In betwixt chores, Emmit's been felling trees out in the land below his cabin. He's notched the logs and piled them all together. Now that he's got enough logs for a cow barn, the men'll come and help him build it and put on a roof. And if it ain't too dry, they'll burn the brush from off the trees and there'll be a grand big bonfire."

"Then comes the fun part," interrupted Walter Keller. "After they're all done, we'll have us a play party with a big bate of food and singing games nigh on to midnight."

"That sounds very nice," Erin said. "I'll look forward to it."

There was a noise by the door. Will Witbeck and Rabe Hinkle had snatched Sariah's lunch pail and were throwing it back and forth between them. Erin forced herself to speak in a pleasant tone.

"Boys, please stop that and take your seats. Everyone, sit down so I can take roll."

The children went reluctantly to their desks. Everyone was present except Enlo and Winifred. Erin was going to have to make a visit to Reverend Butler's to resolve the problem with Enlo, but she was not sorry to get a reprieve from him.

Rabe Hinkle raised a grimy hand.

"Yes, Rabe?"

"Would it discomfort you if I put another log on the fire, Teacher? It's a mite cold back here by the window."

"Go ahead, Rabe."

Perhaps Erin was making some progress, after all. Rabe had never raised his hand before for anything, and he had spoken politely.

Rabe took some wood from the box and carefully put it in the stove. He seemed to take quite a while to situate the log.

"That's fine," Erin said. "Please take your seat, Rabe."

Erin had turned to write on the blackboard, and didn't see that Rabe had smuggled a glowing piece of kindling back to his desk. As she reached up to print a spelling word, five loud explosions popped in the back of the room. Erin jumped around in time to see Ameriky Reynolds dancing in the aisle, slapping sparks out of his back pocket.

Erin heard a few uneasy snickers from the back of the room. The rest of the children waited anxiously to see what their teacher would do next. Ameriky wasn't hurt, but the sparks had burned several holes in the back of his overalls.

"Rabe Hinkle, you come up here this instant," Erin said, so angry she could barely speak.

Rabe's eyes opened wide and he walked forward.

"What did you put in Ameriky's pocket?" Erin demanded. Rabe shifted his feet and stared at the floor. "Rabe, you will tell me this instant what made all that noise!"

"Firecrackers," he murmured. "But they wasn't mine. I didn't bring 'em."

"Ameriky could have been badly burned by that prank, Rabe, to say nothing of the lack of respect you showed for your school. Now, you just march yourself home for the rest of the day, and don't come back unless you can abide by my rules. If you ever try such nonsense again, I'll take a switch to your behind."

Rabe hesitated a moment, then he walked out the door. Erin wasn't finished yet. "I want to know who brought those firecrackers to school. Whoever did it might as well confess. There'll be no recess or dinner until you do. We'll just sit here and wait."

After a few minutes, a hand went up on the boys' side of the room. "Yes, Ludie?"

"They was mine, Teacher. I never thought about them hurting nobody, though, honest."

"I see. Well, I think you'd better go on home too and tell your parents what you've done."

Ludie picked up his books and walked out the door like a whipped puppy.

"What is wrong with you children?" Erin cried. "I came here wanting to teach you, wanting to share all the wonderful things in these books, and what do you do? You play pranks and giggle and whisper. Don't you think I have any feelings? Don't you want to learn?"

Erin looked at the children's faces. "It's time for recess," she said. "Class is dismissed."

She sat down at her desk, vaguely aware of the children's raucous play outside the window, blinking back tears. She didn't hear the light footsteps behind her. Grubby fingers touched her hand, and then Sariah Hinkle put her arms around Erin's neck.

"I'm sorry for our orneriness, Teacher," she said.

Erin felt her anger begin to melt away. "That's all right, Sariah. We're all ornery sometimes."

"Even you, Teacher?"

"Especially me. But do you know what, Sariah?"

"What, Teacher?"

"There's Someone who always loves us no matter how ornery we are."

"You mean God."

"That's right. God loves us very much, and He'll always be there to forgive us and take care of us."

"My mama says that, too. Last spring Mama and me prayed and I asked Jesus to come into my heart. Mama says that God loves my daddy and Rabe and everybody."

"She's right, Sariah, and He wants us to love each other, too."

Sariah's small face was thoughtful. "Teacher? Don't it jist make you feel warm all over?" She jumped down and scampered out the door.

ten

The day of the barn raising began with a sunny sky. Tucker hitched up the horses and helped Mattie and Erin into the wagon. Mattie balanced her "Scripture cake" in her lap on the wagon seat, while Douglas and Erin held on to a big pan of beans in the back. Jube and Ben had left earlier on foot. Tucker turned the horses off the road onto a rough wagon trail that led up hill through a pine grove, then plunged down among dense stands of hickory and walnut.

The Stiles' home was the smallest that Erin had seen yet, with huge old oak trees surrounding it on every side. Tucker pulled the horses up in the yard and set the brake.

"Well, Preacher," he said. "You ready to do a man's day of work?"

"As ready as you are, Tucker. Just show me where to start."

"You can take the tool box over to where the men are working. I'll be there directly."

The women were already busy in Rose's cabin. It would be dinnertime soon, and the men would be hungry. Plank tables had been set up in the yard to accommodate the crowd.

Widow Puckett was waiting for them on the porch. "Mattie Cotter, did you go and bring that Scripture cake of yours? You know I've been wanting to learn the secret of that recipe for ages."

"Ain't no secret, Widder, jist a little of this 'n' that." Mattie nodded towards Erin. "Erin helped me bake this one."

Rose was busy in her tiny kitchen. Erin hadn't seen Rose for several weeks, since she had reached her period of confinement and had been staying home from church. All this extra work must be hard on her in her condition; she still looked like a child herself.

"Good morning, Rose," Erin said. "How can I help?"

"I appreciate the offer, Miz Erin, but everything's nearly done. I was jist fussing over the pots. We're gitting ready to go out

91

and look at the working. Asa Keller says he can raise a barn wall faster than anybody, and he's taking on all comers."

They went out to the field where the men were working. Some men worked in teams, lifting the notched logs into place. Others worked to one side, cutting wood shingles for the roof. Douglas had been teamed with Clay Reynolds and John Witbeck. Erin couldn't help but notice the strained look on Douglas' face as he attacked yet another log.

The women returned to the cabin, and after checking the pots on the stove, they picked up the piecework they had brought with them and found seats on the few chairs in the room, or on Emmit and Rose's bed. Mattie had told Erin to bring some sort of stitchery to do, so she pulled out a hook and some thread from her bag and began to crochet a doily.

"How pretty, Miz Erin," exclaimed Becky Keller. "I always admired crocheting, but I never did learn."

"Of course that kind of work is fine," sniffed Widow Puckett, "But a farm wife don't have much use for such fancies. I taught my Bessie here to quilt and sew and do such work as a country woman needs to know about." The Widow Puckett peered up at Erin from her work. "I heared you had some trouble at the school this week, Miz Corbett."

"Oh, well, it was just a schoolboy prank," Erin said. "Nothing to be alarmed about."

"Ludie told me about them firecrackers," said Mrs. Stiles. "We're right sorry for what happened. He ought to have knowed better."

"I hear the younguns is getting a little out of hand, cutting didoes right in the middle of their lessons," said the Widow.

"We've had a few discipline problems," admitted Erin. "But I am sure as we come to know one another better, things will settle down."

"If 'twas up to me," the Widow snapped, "I'd settle it with a little peach tree tea and some old-fashioned schooling instead of all these new-fangled ideas."

"Widder, let Erin alone," Mattie said. "She ain't hardly had time to git started yet." Erin gave Mattie a grateful glance. Mattie put her sewing back in her basket and got up. "We best be gitting dinner," she said. "The menfolks will be ready to eat soon."

The women followed Mattie to the stove and began to dish up the meal and carry it outside to the table. The table was crowded with dishes: ham, chicken, fried rabbit, squirrel stew, beans, hominy, cornbread, biscuits and jelly, sweet potatoes, loaves of fresh bread, pickles, sauerkraut, and applesauce. For dessert, there was Mattie's Scripture cake and a dozen dried-apple pies.

The men sat at the table while the women poured coffee and refilled their dishes. Never had Erin seen so much food consumed so quickly. When she reached over Douglas' shoulder to fill his cup, she noticed how pale his face was.

"You tired?" she asked quietly.

"A little. Don't say anything. They're watching to see if I can keep up with them."

The men filled their plates and filled them again. Then, one by one, they began to make their way back toward the field.

"You about ready, Preacher?" Jube asked.

Douglas stood up stiffly and stretched his arms. "I suppose so, Jube. Let's get it done."

The afternoon progressed much as the morning. After the women and children ate at the second table, they cleaned up and set the leftovers back for the meal to follow. The women sat down to more hand work and conversation.

Erin learned that Reverend Butler was expected back sometime today from a revival in Palmer, and he was anxious to get Enlo back in school. The ladies also let it slip that Mr. Hinkle was angry with Erin for sending Rabe home. The Hinkles were not at the working today, Erin supposed, because of Narcissy's advanced pregnancy.

Since the barn was not very large, the men finished early in the afternoon. The children made their way in from playing in the woods, and families soon were enjoying a relaxed supper in the yard. Douglas looked drawn and tired as he sat down on the quilt beside Erin.

"Are you all right?" she asked.

"Yes, but I don't think I'll be moving very fast in the morning."

Jube and Tucker looked none the worse for their day's work.
Tucker took a hefty bite of ginger cake and washed it down
with spring water. "Preacher, I 'spect you're about wore out,"
he said. "You done a fair job of work today."

"I take that as a high compliment coming from you, Tucker."
Douglas leaned closer to Erin and said softly in her ear, "Would
you walk out back with me? I would like to talk to you alone."

Erin glanced around at the others. She found Tucker's knowing eyes resting on her face, and her chin raised. "All right,
Douglas. If you're sure you wouldn't rather rest."

Douglas shook his head and got to his feet. They strolled
through the trees, then leaned against an outcropping of rocks
behind Emmit's new barn. "I'm very proud of you," Erin said.
"You didn't give up, even though they deliberately gave you
the hardest jobs."

"Well, it's over now. How was your day?"

"Oh, as Mattie would say, it was 'tolerable.' Why did you
want to talk to me?"

Douglas leaned toward her and placed his hands on hers.
"This isn't the way I planned it, but with your school and the
church work, I've hardly had a moment alone with you." He
fidgeted with his shirt collar and cleared his throat.

"What is it, Douglas? Is something wrong?"

"No, no, it isn't that. I just envisioned this happening in a
more appropriate setting, certainly not in a barnyard."

"What do you mean, Douglas?"

"That first day, when we met at the depot, I thought you
were the most beautiful creature I'd ever seen. In the time we've
been here, I've found that you're not only lovely, but also a most
gracious young woman, someone well suited to the ministry, and
someone deserving of a lifestyle fitting a fine lady. I can offer
you that sort of life, Erin. When I complete my assignment
here, my father has promised to arrange for me to pastor one of

the largest churches in Chicago. I'd like for you to be my helpmate in that work, Erin. . .I am asking you to marry me."

Erin sat quietly, not knowing what to do or say.

"Erin, do you have an answer?"

"You've caught me by surprise, Douglas. Perhaps the Lord did bring us together here. Your proposal is very flattering. . ."

"Then accept it!"

"Would you give me some time to pray about it?" asked Erin. "I want to be absolutely sure."

Douglas smiled broadly. "Of course. Erin, I know this is right. We could be married next summer, just as soon as our assignment ends here."

"Well, I suppose I hadn't necessarily intended to stay here more than one term, and we would be serving in another church. But first, they'd have to find another teacher to take my place."

"I'm sure they can find someone. Erin, we will have a wonderful life. The church I will pastor has a beautiful parsonage, and I'll show you such a time in Chicago. With you at my side, I'll be the envy of every man in town."

"Imagine, our own beautiful home. It is what I've always wanted."

Douglas pulled Erin toward him and kissed her. Then his arms encircled her and he kissed her again, more insistently. So many emotions tumbled inside of her, but one thing Erin knew, she liked being in Douglas' arms. Reluctantly, though, she pulled herself away.

"Douglas, someone might see. We must continue to be discreet in public," she said.

"That will prove difficult, I assure you."

Douglas reached for Erin again, but bare feet rustled in the leaves behind them. Erin whirled around to find Ben staring at her. His face showed a mixture of disbelief and betrayal.

"Mattie sent me to come fetch you," he said. "The singing games is about to start." He spun around and ran off to the front of the house.

"Do you suppose he saw us?" Douglas asked.

"I'm afraid so," said Erin. "I'll talk to him. I hope I can make him understand."

The men had built the brush from the logs into a huge pile, and now, as the sun sank behind the trees, they lit the bonfire. The children danced around the flickering light, and the grownups soon joined them in a circle. Someone began to sing, and then the others joined in, the sad, sweet ballads rising into the growing darkness.

Erin stood between Tucker and Mattie at the edge of the circle. The singers' voices changed now, became faster and happier, and someone began to clap. Erin discovered that she was patting her foot to the rhythms, and soon she too was singing.

"Miz Erin," Tucker said softly in her ear, "I'm jist beginning to think we might make a country girl out of you yet, jist maybe, mind you." She looked up into his firelit face and saw the warmth in his eyes. "I been thinking on it," he said. "Maybe it's time you and me come to an understanding."

Erin smiled. "You mean a truce?"

"You might say that, I reckon. I expect I've been a little hard on you now and again."

"I'd like it very much if we could be friends, Tucker."

Tucker's deep bass voice joined the others on the chorus of a new song called "Weevily Wheat":

> "Oh, don't you think she's a pretty little miss?,
> and don't you think she's clever,
> and don't you think that she and I
> would make a match forever?"

The song ended, and Tucker led Erin back to the wagon where Mattie had left a crock full of apple cider. Tucker handed her a cup and she drank down the golden liquid.

"This is good," Erin said. "So much singing dries your throat." She looked over her shoulder at the lively circle around the fire, and she laughed. "I can't imagine what the headmistress at the orphanage would think. She was very strict when it came to social gatherings. I'm sure she'd find this one much too boisterous for her taste."

"Well, regardless, I'd allow as she did a fair to middling job of raising you up right."

"Thank you, Tucker." Erin looked around the yard. "I wonder what has happened to Douglas."

"I expect the Preacher can take care of hisself, least for a few minutes, anyway."

"Just the same, I shouldn't have abandoned him."

"Like as not he's over buttering up the Widder and her man-hungry daughter."

"Tucker, couldn't you and Douglas try to get along? Really, if you would give him a chance, Douglas is very nice. You saw how hard he worked today. And he is a man of God, after all."

Tucker stared down at Erin. "Appears to me you got more than a passing interest in the Preacher."

"Well, I. . .it isn't that," she stammered. "I would defend Douglas even if we weren't. . ."

"Weren't what?" Tucker's gray eyes pierced through Erin's. "You're fixing to marry that hoon yock, aren't you?"

Erin looked away from him. "I haven't given him a definite answer."

"You're jist enough of a ninny to say yes."

"As a matter of fact, I might. But, even if I did, we don't intend to announce it for some time, and I'll finish the school year regardless, so I'd appreciate it if you would keep this to yourself."

"You got no more business to marry that city boy than the man in the moon. You can do better, Miz Erin."

"My personal life is none of your concern, Mr. Gillam, and I'll thank you to keep your nose out of my affairs."

Tucker shook his head. "I might a knowed, you ain't no different from the rest. There ain't no city woman alive that wants anything but fancy geegaws and an easy life. You figure one year here with us poor crackers pays all your dues? Don't you fret 'bout my keeping your secret. That ain't the kind of news I would care to pass on."

eleven

The mood was decidedly unpleasant at breakfast on Monday morning. Ben ate silently, casting angry glances toward Douglas and Erin between bites. Tucker sat at the head of the table, grumpily mixing molasses and grits together on his plate. Jube kept to himself, still groggy from the late hours he had kept over the weekend. Mattie and Douglas were the only cheerful souls in the room, and they tried their best to encourage a polite conversation.

"Good attendance yesterday, don't you think, Mattie?" Douglas asked.

"Right smart, and after a party night, too."

Jube sipped loudly from his saucer, and then set it down to cool. "Tucker, you reckon I ought to check on the Widder this morning?"

"You might, she was real upset about losing them chickens."

"I don't blame her," Mattie said. "It's shameful to think a body can't leave her place for an evening without some outlaw sneaking in and stealing the livestock right smack out of the yard."

"I have some time this morning," Douglas offered. "If you like, I can ride out and see if I can find any signs of the intruder."

Tucker hardly looked up from his plate. "Naw, Preacher, I expect you best leave that to Jube and me. But if it's work you're looking for, Mattie's real busy in the kitchen this time of year."

Erin set her milk glass down loudly on the table and glared at Tucker, but Mattie jumped in before she could say anything.

"Tucker, you're as tetchous as an old sow this morning. You know I wouldn't let the Preacher, nor any other man, in that kitchen long as I run this house."

"If you haven't any plans for this morning, Douglas, I could use your help at the school. This might be the last day of nice weather, and I thought I would take the children on a little picnic in the woods. It would help to have another adult along to keep them all together."

"It would be my pleasure, Erin."

Erin smiled a pointedly charming smile at Douglas. "Thank you," she said. "Maybe some of the boys who have been causing trouble will think twice about misbehaving with a man present."

Tucker looked up from his meal. "You been having more troubles at the school, besides that ruckus between Ben and Enlo?"

Erin hesitated. "Well, yes, some. Mostly just talking out and playing pranks. Nothing serious."

"What pranks?" Douglas asked. "You haven't said anything about pranks before."

"It's nothing, really, toads in my desk drawers, burrs on my chair, things like that."

"Did you whup the boys that played these pranks?" asked Tucker.

"No, I didn't. I don't believe in whipping children."

"You see, Tucker, the finest schools of education no longer condone corporal punishment," Douglas explained.

"Huh," Tucker scoffed. "Your finer schools might change their minds if they knowed some of the younguns around here."

"J. H. Pestalozzi says that learning must first be based in mutual friendship between student and teacher," Erin said. "When that relationship is established, education can begin. A good teacher does not have discipline problems."

"Horse apples!" cried Tucker. "That J. H. Pester feller ain't never taught at Lost Crick. Like as not he's some old goober out of a book that's been dead for fifty years or more."

"Now, wait a moment," said Douglas. "I hardly think you are qualified to second guess Erin's methods. She has a teaching certificate, after all."

Tucker ignored Douglas. "What about this here picnic? Are you so far ahead with your lessons that you can afford to take the day off to play in the woods?"

"We are not taking the day off. J. H. Pestalozzi says. . ."

"Oh, corn, here she goes again with that Pester feller," Tucker moaned.

"J. H. Pestalozzi says that children can learn many things from nature. They need more than just schoolwork and chores, you know."

Tucker grunted, unconvinced, and went back to eating his breakfast.

"My methods may seem strange to you, but I just want these children to have as progressive an education as any child in St. Louis," Erin said.

"Jist as long as you ain't having a play day," Tucker conceded. "But, I still think more could be learned in the schoolhouse."

"I think Erin knows what she is doing," Douglas said.

"I don't recollect asking for your opinion, Preacher," said Tucker. "Miz Erin, I don't care if you stand on your head and spit buckshot, if you think that will make you a better teacher, but I expect you to put a stop to any tom-foolery going on and learn them children what they come there for."

"I will handle the children, Mr. Gillam."

"See that you do, Miz Corbett."

Erin stood up and pushed her chair in firmly under the table. "I need to start for school, or I'll be late," she said. "Ben, would you please walk along with me this morning and carry that box of slates that came from the mission board? It's too heavy for me."

Ben looked up at Erin, clearly annoyed. "I reckon I'd ruther not."

Tucker threw down the napkin from under his chin. "Benjamin Daniel Gillam, either you haul yourself out of that chair right now and help Miz Erin, or I'll guarantee you won't be setting down for your supper."

Ben sat still.

"You hear me, boy?" Tucker bellowed.

After a moment's consideration, Ben gave up the struggle. "Yes, sir," he said. "I'll git my books."

"Thank you, Ben. Douglas, if you'd come to the school around nine-thirty, I believe we'll be ready to go."

No matter how fast Erin walked on the way to school, Ben managed to keep a good amount of road between them. "Ben, please wait," Erin called. "Please. . .I want to talk to you."

Ben stopped and looked down at the road while Erin hurried to catch up with him. "I want to git on to the schoolhouse," he said. "Got some tradin' to do with Ameriky."

"I see. Well, maybe you could spare me just a minute. Ben, I know you're upset with me. I don't blame you. It must seem as if I've told you a boldface lie."

"You did! You said you weren't sweet on the Preacher, then I come and see you two kissing right spang in the broad daylight."

"I'm sorry about that, Ben. It was impulsive of us. But I wasn't 'sweet' on Reverend Teterbaugh at first. At least, he and I had no understanding between each other at that time."

"Meanin' you got this 'understanding' now?"

"Yes, Ben, I suppose we do."

Ben clenched his fists and turned away. "It ain't fair! You gonna up and marry that Preacher and he'll take you out of here jist as quick as he can go. You said you was staying; you told us you had plans for our school."

"Ben, I won't leave before the school term is up, I promise. Nothing is settled yet, anyway. I'm sorry. I didn't mean to lie to you, but sometimes you can't anticipate where life will take you. Perhaps God brought Douglas into my life because He intends for us to serve Him together."

"Maybe God works that way for you. All I know is, He ain't never brought nobody into my life; He jist takes them out."

Ben got a firm grip on his bundle and ran up the road to the school. The sunshine seemed dimmer, somehow, as Erin followed him up the hill.

Inside the schoolhouse, Erin took roll, noting that Enlo and Winifred were absent again. Erin was relieved that she would not have to contend with Enlo on their hike.

Douglas appeared in the doorway. "Reverend Teterbaugh, come right in," Erin said. "Class, I have a surprise for you. We're fortunate to have the Reverend as our guest today. I'm sure you will want to show him what a well-behaved class you can be." Douglas smiled at the children.

"All right, I believe we're ready. You older boys will take the lead. Keep your eyes and ears open. I want you to look at these woods as if you were seeing them for the very first time."

The children streamed out of the schoolhouse door and scrambled up the hill, with Douglas and Erin following close behind. As they walked along the winding trail, the children pointed out tracks of opossum, raccoons, deer, and even a bear, who obviously did not know he was supposed to be hibernating.

As they crested a hill, the children jumped from log to log and ducked between the trees. The boys swung from grapevines like young monkeys. Dry leaves crunched beneath their feet as they darted in and out, calling as they ran. Sariah Hinkle and Annie Witbeck skipped along hand in hand, wrapped up in the sweet joy of childhood friendship.

"They're having such a good time. I almost hate to spoil it by making them start their lessons."

"If you don't, Tucker will never let you hear the end of it," Douglas said. He touched Erin's hand. "Teacher, you look beautiful this morning."

Erin pulled her hand away and smiled. "Stop your flattery and come along before we lose the children."

Just then, a scream echoed through the trees. Erin looked ahead and saw a cluster of terrified children frozen around Sariah Hinkle. Ben ran up with a tree branch in his hand, raised it above his head, and sent it crashing down just a few inches from where Sariah lay. Erin ran toward the children as

Ben repeatedly thrashed the ground with his stick.

"Ben, what is it?" Erin cried.

Ben bent over Sariah, who was now sobbing loudly. The bludgeoned carcass of a large copper-colored snake lay next to her in the fallen leaves. Ben had both hands on the child, trying to keep her still. Erin sat down and pulled Sariah into her lap. Blood trickled down from two red fang marks just below her right knee. Erin had never felt so helpless in her life.

"Ben, run and find Tucker," she ordered. "He'll know what to do. Tell him to hurry."

"Yes'm. It'd save time if the Preacher could tote her back to the road. We could meet you with the team."

"Fine, Ben; we'll meet you. Now go!"

"Don't let her thrash about none," Ben called over his shoulder. "It makes the pizen work faster."

Douglas bent over to inspect Sariah's leg. "Should we try to cleanse the wound or cover it with something?"

"I don't know, Douglas. I've never seen a snakebite before."

Sariah moved restlessly in Erin's lap. "Teacher, it hurts."

"I know, honey. Ben went to get help. You try and be still."

Douglas carefully lifted Sariah in his arms. Erin looked around for Sariah's brother. "Rabe, run and tell your father that Sariah's been hurt. Tell him we'll take her to the Gillam place."

Rabe turned without a word and ran in the direction of his cabin.

What had been a pleasant walk a minute ago seemed like an endless trek now as Douglas hurried back over the trail with Sariah. Erin moved along with the rest of the children, praying silently all the way.

Tucker and Ben were already driving the buckboard toward them as they came down off the hill. Tucker jerked the horses to a stop and jumped down. He took Sariah and carried her to the back of the wagon; she looked like a rag doll in his arms. Tucker gently laid her down, then he reached into his pocket and pulled out his knife.

"This'll hurt a mite, punkin', but we got to git it done."

Sariah nodded. Erin watched in horror as Tucker took a firm hold on the child's leg and cut an X shape over each fang mark with his knife. Sariah blanched and bit her lip, but she remained quiet. Tucker leaned over, put his mouth to the wound and sucked, then he turned and spat the blood on the ground.

"Preacher, you got a clean kerchief?" Tucker asked.

Douglas fumbled in his pockets and handed his handkerchief to Tucker. Tucker smiled at Sariah. "You're a brave little gal. We'll git you back to my place and Mattie'll have something to make you feel better. You jist hang on a little while longer."

Tucker tied the handkerchief on tightly, just above the swelling on Sariah's leg.

"Miz Erin, you ride back here with her," he said. "Keep her still and prop up her leg so it won't throb as much."

Erin climbed up over the back of the wagon and turned to see the rest of the children waiting by the side of the road. "School is dismissed, children," she said. "You may go home."

Sariah and Erin settled down on some horse blankets in the wagon bed. Tucker was already back on the seat with Ben.

Mattie was waiting in the yard when they pulled up. Sariah seemed quieter now; she didn't cry out as much as when she had first been bitten.

"How bad is it?" Mattie asked. Tucker looked at her, but he did not answer aloud.

"You bring that child into my room," Mattie ordered. "I got the bed all ready."

Tucker carried Sariah in and laid her down. Sariah's forehead felt cold and clammy, and her leg was swelling at an alarming rate. She began to shiver, and Mattie covered her with a blanket. Then Mattie took charge.

"Tucker, we'll need the medicine jug and turpentine and some clean rags. You better bring me an extry cover, too. Ben, you haul me in some water and set it on the stove, then git to your chores. Ain't nothin' more you can do."

They both left to do as Mattie asked. Mattie stayed next to the child, stroking her and speaking softly. There was a love in Mattie like Erin had never seen in anyone before.

Tucker returned with a jug and a small drinking glass. Mattie removed the cork and poured out a few swallows of clear liquid.

"Drink this down," she said. "It don't taste good, but it'll ease the hurt."

Sariah drank it, but it made her cough. "It burns, Miz Mattie."

"I know, angel, it'll pass. You try and sleep."

Mattie put the child's leg up on a pillow and cleaned the wound with the turpentine Tucker brought. "Erin, I'd appreciate it if you'd make up a fresh pot of coffee and see to dinner. We got a long day ahead of us and likely some extry mouths to feed."

"I'll do my best, Mattie, but I'm not much of a cook. You will call me if I can help with Sariah, won't you?"

"Yes, child. Now, don't you fret, I've doctored more than one snakebite in my time."

Tucker followed Erin into the kitchen and began building up the fire in the cookstove. There was a strained silence, until Erin finally got up the courage to ask what was on her mind.

"Tucker, you said before that snakebites usually weren't fatal unless the victims were very young or very old. Is Sariah old enough. . .I mean. . .Sariah's not going to die, is she?"

Tucker put in one more piece of kindling and replaced the lid. He was choosing his words carefully. "It ain't easy to say. Copperheads don't commonly give a mortal bite, but Ben said it was a big snake. From the swelling, I'd say she got a goodly dose of pizen. Snakes don't oft times strike this time of year. I guess she must have stepped right on top of him. I reckon we'll jist have to wait this one out."

"But surely the doctor can give her something."

"Mattie done give her about all there is to give."

"There's got to be more we can do! We're so isolated here. Perhaps I could send a wire to St. Louis for a specialist."

"By the time anyone could git here, it'd be all over, one way or the other. Jube went to get Doc Stone. Doc'll pull her through if anybody can. If you're so direct minded to do something, why don't you find that Preacher and see if you can't git him to go out to the Hinkle place. Narcissy's gonna need some help to git her through this, what with her time nigh due."

❧

It took Jube several hours to locate Dr. Stone, who had been out on a call near Picayune Ridge. The doctor arrived at sundown on a tired looking sorrel mare. He dismounted and took a leather satchel from the saddle horn. The doctor's shoulders drooped as he walked, and his black suit coat was shiny at the elbows. Mattie said he had been riding these isolated trails for nearly twenty-five years. He looked accustomed to little sleep and long rides through dark woods.

Dr. Stone came into the bedroom, set his hat on Mattie's dressing table, and went to work. Sariah's leg was doubled in size from thigh to toe. The bite area had turned blue-black, like a bad bruise, and had swollen hard to the touch. The doctor felt Sariah's head and looked into her eyes. The child seemed only half conscious, staring passively as the doctor examined her.

"Any nausea, Mattie?"

"Not yet. She started to chill, but I give her some medicine whiskey and it seemed to help."

"She's been awfully thirsty," Erin said. The doctor looked up, aware for the first time that there was a stranger in the room.

"Adam Stone," Mattie said, "This here's Miz Erin Corbett, the new missionary teacher. Sariah got bit whilst they was out on a school picnic."

"How do you do, Doctor."

The doctor nodded. "Pleased t'meet you." He turned his attention back to Sariah. He opened his bag and handed Mattie a small paper envelope. "Give her one of these powders in some water. We'll try to keep her fever down, if we can."

Mattie took the medicine from the doctor. "You got to git to another call, or you planning to stay on a while?"

Dr. Stone looked at the pale child who slept fitfully next to him on the bed. He rubbed his chin with his fingers and pulled at his ear. "I reckon I'll stay on a while. I don't like the sound of her breathing. We won't be out of the woods on this one for a while yet, Mattie."

"I reckoned not, Adam," Mattie said softly.

There were footsteps on the porch and the front door slammed. "Where's my Sariah?" a voice demanded.

Erin stepped out into the parlor and saw Seth Hinkle. By his swagger, it looked as if he had more than his share of liquor in him.

"Rabe says you got my Sariah here. I come to git her."

"She is in here, Mr. Hinkle, but she is in no condition. . ."

"Don't tell me about no condition." He pushed past Erin and stopped inside the door. "Who told you to call for the Doc? I ain't paying for no doctor. You ain't got no right to call for him without my say so."

"You needn't worry 'bout the money," Mattie said. "Tucker'll take care of the Doc. Do you want t'know about your little'n, or are you too drunk to care?"

A faint light of awareness gleamed in Mr. Hinkle's piggish eyes. "Is she ailin' that bad, Doc?"

The doctor rubbed his chin thoughtfully. "Seth, it's a bad bite. I'd be hard put to say how it'll come out. I'll do my best for her, I give you my word on that."

Mr. Hinkle staggered toward Erin. "It's your fault," he said. "You with your high falutin' city teaching ways. You're the one what said I should send my younguns to your school. Well, I sent 'em and look what come of it."

Dr. Stone turned around to look at Mr. Hinkle. "Seth, there are snakes all over these hills. Sariah could have gotten bit going to the outhouse."

"No, it's all the Teacher's fault. . .her and that dandy of a preacher they got."

Mr. Hinkle's words burned like hot coals. He had spoken aloud what Erin had dared not think since the moment Sariah had been bitten.

"And I'll tell you another thing," Mr. Hinkle said. "You let her git bit, you can jist take care of her. A man's only meant to bear so much. My woman's about to birth again and she won't hardly git up out of bed herself. You can jist keep Sariah here."

"Seth Hinkle, you're drunk," said Dr. Stone. "Now you git on out of here, or I'll throw you out myself." The doctor took a deep breath. "Go sober up and take care of Narcissy. We'll send word when there's a change."

Mr. Hinkle put on his torn felt hat and staggered out of the bedroom. He stopped unsteadily at the parlor door and pointed his finger in Erin's face. "If my girl dies, it's on your head, missy."

Erin looked at Sariah lying motionless underneath the covers, and then she ran blindly through the back door, past the springhouse to the apple grove. She flung herself on the ground and cried until no more tears would come, but she was no more at peace than before. Getting to her feet, she brushed at the stains on her skirt from the wind-thrown apples that lay rotting on the ground beneath her. "If my girl dies. . ." The words tumbled over and over in Erin's mind.

She couldn't think of it anymore. She wouldn't. She would think of something else. The least she could do was to make good on her promise to Mattie and get dinner. She walked stiffly back to the house.

Tucker was standing at the stove with the coffeepot in his hand.

"How is Sariah?" Erin asked.

"Holding on. Doc's with her. Mattie went over to check on Narcissy. I was fixing to take the Doc some supper."

"I'll do it; I promised Mattie. Hand me the coffeepot, would you, please?"

Tucker handed Erin the pot, and she poured the dark liquid into Mattie's china cup.

"You all right?" Tucker asked.

"Yes, I'm fine." Erin knew her red eyes and disheveled appearance were evidence to the contrary, but she had no energy to discuss it with Tucker now.

"I reckon I'll git some chores done. I'll be in the barn if you need anything."

"All right, Tucker, thank you."

"Miz Erin?"

"Yes?"

"Doc told me what Seth Hinkle said to you. Don't pay him no mind. He talks through a jug most of the time. I know I come down on you about taking them children on the picnic, but that snake could have been anywheres. There's no reason to blame yourself."

"Thank you, Tucker."

Erin took the tray to the sick room. Dr. Stone was sitting in a straight chair next to the bed, watching Sariah. Erin put the tray down and sat on the side of the bed. Sariah's forehead was hot. Her leg was swollen and red, and the wound area was now covered with open blisters.

"Is she doing all right, Doctor?"

The doctor looked at Erin and rubbed his hand over his chin. "I'd hoped we'd not have such a rough time. Copperheads generally are the lesser of evils with snakes around here, but she's having a bad reaction. I just don't know."

"Surely you'll be able to tell something soon. By morning we should know, shouldn't we?"

Dr. Stone put his calloused hand over Erin's. "I'm afraid the effects of the venom don't reach their peak until the third or fourth day."

"Four days? She can't stand this for four days."

Dr. Stone took a wet cloth from the basin and wiped Sariah's face. "It will get worse," he said. "The venom affects the blood, makes it so it won't clot. Along with the fever, there'll be tissue damage, her gums may bleed, might be blood in the urine and stools, and breathing trouble. There's also the chance of infection in the wound itself."

"Can't you do anything, give her something? There must be a medicine. If it's a matter of money. . ."

The doctor got up from his chair and walked to the window. "It isn't about money. There simply isn't anything to give. I read where some New York doctors are working on a serum . . .maybe in a few years. . .but not now. All we can do is try and keep her comfortable."

Sariah stirred, and Dr. Stone took advantage of the opportunity to put a teaspoon of water into her mouth.

"Do you believe in prayer, Doctor?"

The doctor placed the spoon back in the glass. "As long as I've been tending folks, I'd be a fool not to. I've seen the impossible too many times."

For the first time since the accident, Erin felt a surge of hope. She needed to pray. God wouldn't let this beautiful child die if she could just pray hard enough. She determined to spend every spare minute lifting Sariah up to God in prayer.

❦

The doctor came by as often as he could between calls, but after the first night, Mattie and Erin took over caring for Sariah. Douglas volunteered to fill in for Erin at the school until Sariah was better, and she agreed. Erin could think of nothing else but Sariah. She made a constant effort to pray for the child.

The nights were the hardest, when time seemed to crawl, an endless cycle of cold compresses, drinks, and changing of night clothes and bed linens. On the third night, Sariah seemed to improve a little, and Mattie agreed to leave Erin with the child while she got some sleep in Ben's room. It had turned cold, so Erin wrapped up in a quilt and settled into Mattie's rocking chair.

The next thing Erin knew, someone was sitting on the edge of Sariah's bed. Startled, she leaned forward in the chair and tried to get up, but her feet were caught in the coverlet.

"Set still," Tucker said. "She's all right. I jist put a fresh poultice on her leg." He looked over at Erin. "Why don't you go on to bed. You're tuckered out."

"No, I'm all right. Besides, I don't want Mattie to miss another night's sleep."

"Mattie's taught me a trick or two about nursing sick folks. I'll set up with her. You ain't had no more sleep than Mattie. You go on."

Erin knew she would not be able to stay awake all night. "All right," she said. "But only for a few hours. Wake me around two o'clock and I'll spell you."

"Fair enough. Now you go get some rest."

Tucker bent over Sariah and carefully sponged her face. For such a rough looking man, he had a gentle touch. Erin decided that Sariah would be in good hands. She stumbled to her room and fell asleep at once.

ፙ

Erin opened bleary eyes to a room full of light. The hands of the little brass clock showed it was after nine o'clock. Why hadn't anyone awakened her? She put on her wrapper and hurried out of her room. Tucker and Dr. Stone were drinking coffee at the dining room table, but they both stopped short and stood up when they saw her. The door to Mattie's room was shut tight.

"Why is the door closed?" Erin asked. "Where's Mattie?"

The doctor offered Erin a chair. "Sit down," he said. "There's something we need to tell you."

"Where is Mattie?" Erin insisted.

"I'm afraid we got a sorrow for you," Tucker said.

"Mattie?"

"She's not here," said Tucker. "She and the Preacher went to make a call at the Hinkles'."

Erin ran to Mattie's door and flung it open. There on the bed lay Sariah's still, small body, the lines of pain now erased from her face.

"No! She wasn't supposed to die. . .I prayed! Oh dear Lord, it's my fault. . .it's my fault!"

Through a fog of grief, Erin felt the doctor firmly leading

her to the sofa. Tucker was kneeling down in front of her, so she had to look him in the eyes.

"You listen here," he said. "There wasn't nothing anyone could do. The pizen was jist too much for her. It wasn't nobody's fault."

Tucker's words meant nothing to Erin. If God was just and merciful, why would He let a child like Sariah die? She had prayed for her. Why hadn't God answered? A wave of rage swelled up within her and demanded release.

She pounded her fists into her lap, and when she felt Tucker's hands grip her wrists, she twisted free and began to flail at him. Tucker encircled her in his arms, rocking her back and forth as one would calm a small child. Dr. Stone brought a cup with some bitter-tasting liquid and held it to Erin's lips. Gradually, the storm subsided, as the doctor's medicine blunted her pain. She heard Dr. Stone say, "She'll sleep now."

❧

The funeral took place at two o'clock the next day. Mr. Hinkle had grudgingly agreed to use the schoolhouse for the service since his cabin was so small, but he was adamant about Silas Butler performing both the service at the school and the graveside ceremony in the family plot behind the Hinkles' cabin.

The schoolhouse was packed full as Reverend Butler stepped up on the platform. Sariah lay behind him in a open pine casket lined with white muslin. Just before the service began, Tucker and Dr. Stone helped Narcissy Hinkle to a seat up front by her husband.

Bessie Puckett began the service with a song, but the words held no comfort for Erin, and nothing Reverend Butler said as he continued with Scripture and his sermon helped ease the pain. Emotions were running to a high pitch by the time the mourners lined up to view the body. Erin was glad that Douglas took her arm and hurried her outside.

The congregation waited while the family took their final viewing, then the casket was nailed shut, and everyone began the long walk to the Hinkle cabin. Someone brought out a chair for Narcissy by the graveside. Seth and Rabe stood next to her, but neither father nor son showed the slightest hint of emotion. Mattie held the littlest Hinkle boy in her arms as Reverend Butler moved through the graveside service.

". . .we send her soul to God and commit her body to the ground." Butler threw a handful of dirt into the open grave. "Earth t'earth, dust t'dust, looking forward to the last day and life in the world to come." Reverend Butler stepped away and several of the men began shoveling the dirt into the grave. The congregation sang softly until it was completely filled, then, family by family, they started on their way home.

Douglas and Erin walked back slowly. Neither of them said anything until they reached the house. Douglas stopped outside of the door. "I'm not hungry. I believe I'll go on to bed. You'll be all right?"

"Yes, Douglas. Good night."

Erin went inside, feeling burdened and heavy beyond anything she had ever felt before. The house was quiet. She supposed the men were catching up on chores in the barn. Yellow lamp light flickered out of Mattie's doorway.

"That you, Erin?"

"Yes, Mattie."

"Come here, child."

Erin walked to the door. Mattie was sitting in her rocker with her Bible open in her lap. "Come and set, Erin. I want to talk to you."

"I'm awfully tired, Mattie."

"It's been a day to make a body tuckered, ain't it? Rest yourself there on the side of the bed for a minute."

Erin walked over reluctantly and sat down. Mattie searched her face in a way that made Erin feel as if she could see to the bottom of her soul. "You're hurtin', ain't you, child?"

Tears welled up in Erin's eyes. If only Mattie knew how badly she hurt.

"What is it, Erin? You can tell ole Mattie."

Erin dropped to her knees in front of Mattie's chair. Mattie reached out and gently patted her shoulder while tears rolled down Erin's cheeks.

"Mattie, everything's gone wrong. Tucker was right, this job is too hard for me. I want to go home."

"You got no call to blame yourself about Sariah. It was an accident."

"Maybe. But it wouldn't have happened had I kept the children at the school. Anyway, it's more than that. I've failed as a teacher. I can't even keep discipline in my own classroom. Mattie, . . .I'm not sure I want to be a missionary. I prayed harder for Sariah than I have ever prayed before in my life. Why didn't God answer me?"

Mattie stroked Erin's hair. "He answered you, child. He always does. Sometimes He says yes, sometimes no, and sometimes wait, but He always answers. I reckon this time He jist didn't give you the answer you wanted."

"But it's so unfair. She was just a child."

"I know, honey, I don't understand it either, but I been on this old earth long enough to learn that the Lord's ways ain't our own. We got to learn to leave it to the Master and trust Him for His reasons."

"It wasn't supposed to be like this, Mattie. I had wonderful plans. I thought I could reach those children. But it's no use. I can't go on with it. I just don't have the strength."

Mattie let Erin cry for a moment, then put her hands beneath Erin's chin and lifted her head. "You know, Erin, you're right," she said quietly.

"What?"

"You're right. You can't do this job. You jist ain't got what it takes."

Erin sat up, freshly hurt that Mattie had agreed with her.

"Erin, there ain't nothing good you can do in your own power. None of us can. The sorrowful thing is that most folks live their whole lives and never find that out." Mattie's eyes were full of love as she continued, "You come here with your big city schooling, ready to change us poor country folk every which way."

Erin started to protest, but Mattie held up her hand. "Now, let me finish. There ain't nothing wrong with dreams or edgycation, and heaven knows there's things here that need changed . . . but real changes, they have to come from the inside out."

In her heart, Erin knew Mattie was right. Erin realized, to her embarrassment, that she had almost felt as if she had done God a favor by becoming a missionary. "What do I do now, Mattie?"

"Jist talk to the Lord, child, and tell Him how you feel."

Erin took a deep breath and bowed her head. "Father, I came here thinking I would show these people what being a Christian is all about. Instead, I've made a mess of everything I've done. I can't handle this job; I'm not strong enough. But if You still want to use me. . .if You want to work through me . . .here I am."

Erin felt wrapped up in the heavenly Father's own strong arms. She raised her head and smiled tremulously. "Mattie, do you think the people here would let me have another chance?"

"I reckon they would, but I'll tell you truthful, there's some folks that think you and the Preacher are all store-bought clothes and book learning, and no gumption."

"Well, I can't really blame them for that." Erin thought for a moment. "Would it help if I tried to learn the ways of the people here? What if I were to dress more sensibly, and learned how to cook and do chores? Would that help earn their respect?"

"I reckon it'd be a good way to begin, and I'd be proud to teach you anything you want to know. Listen, Tucker said he was gonna go on with the butchering tomorrow while the moon is full. He'd been putting it off with the funeral and all. I can't think of a better way for you to start learning."

twelve

"Well, look at you, Preacher!" cried Jube. "We might make a farm boy outta you yet."

"Glory," said Tucker. "You givin' up the ministry for the farm? I never thought I'd see you in overalls."

"Have your fun, Tucker, I expected it. Erin talked me into this. She seems to think that we need a better understanding of your customs if we are to have an effective ministry here. So, I am ready to learn all there is to know about butchering swine."

Tucker chuckled. "This really your idea, Miz Erin?"

"Yes, mine and Mattie's. With all that has happened, well... I realized I've been rather arrogant, thinking that people would be impressed with me just because I have a big city education. I know now that I'm going to have to earn their respect. So, I intend to start by learning how to do the work of a farm wife, and Mattie's promised to teach me."

Tucker took all this in with great interest. "That'll bear watching," he said. He pushed himself away from the table. "If you want to learn, let's git at it. We're burning daylight."

Tucker and Ben went to the hog pen and cornered their first victim. Douglas and Erin watched while Tucker crept close and felled the animal by delivering a sharp blow to the back of its head with the blunt side of his ax. Ben helped Tucker hang the pig up by its back legs, then Tucker took out his knife and cut deep into its throat. Erin took a deep breath and swallowed hard as she watched the blood run down on the ground.

Jube's voice came from behind her shoulder. "Don't let it worry you," he said. "That ole pig never felt a thing. Tucker's not one to let no animal suffer."

"Jube, you and the Preacher gonna give us a hand scalding this hog, or you gonna stand and jaw all day?" Tucker asked.

"I'm coming. Don't git your chickens in a flutter."

Jube and Douglas helped carry the hog to a cast iron pot in

116

the yard that was filled with boiling water. The men lifted the animal up and dipped the front half in.

"Careful now," Jube said. "Don't leave it in there too long or the hair will set."

The men laid the carcass out on some clean boards. Jube gave Douglas a knife and showed him how to scrape against the grain of the hair to pull it off.

"Now we're ready to hang this porker up," Jube said. "Ole piggy will hang by his heels jist as nice as you please."

Jube removed the head, and Ben took it into the kitchen, then Tucker pointed to a large tin tub. "Preacher, fetch me that gut basin, if you would."

Douglas dragged the tub over and pushed it under the pig. Tucker cut through the belly skin from one end to the other.

"Miz Erin, if you'd go ask Mattie to git us some pans, we'll be needing them directly," Tucker said. "All right, Preacher, you make sure all the innards go in there, while I make this last cut." Douglas bent down to grip the tub.

When Erin returned, Tucker and Jube were busy cleaning out the carcass and Ben was standing nearby, but Douglas was no where in sight.

"Here are the pans, Tucker," she said. "Where's Douglas?"

The men looked at one another. Erin thought she detected a gleam of amusement in their eyes.

"Well," Tucker said, "I ain't for certain, but I suspect that he's out back of the barn losing his breakfast."

"If he is ill, don't you think you ought to go find him?"

"Now don't git your feathers ruffled," Tucker said. "I'll go after him by and by, if he don't show up on his own. He'll be all right. He ain't the first man to have his stomach turned by butchering."

Erin wanted to tell them how mean they were being, how much she resented them putting Douglas through this, but she held her tongue. They weren't asking him to do anything they weren't doing themselves.

The kitchen was filled with every available pot and basin.

There was a pot on the stove for rendering lard, another for boiling the hogs' heads, and a pan sat on the table for scraps that would be chopped into sausage. The entrails were set to soak in salt water and were cooked as time allowed. The men cut up the larger pieces, the hams, shoulders, and roasts, and salted them down for storage in the smoke house. The smaller cuts were sent into the kitchen. Then the whole process would begin again on another hog until finally all four had been butchered. Everything had to be done quickly while the meat was still warm so that it would not spoil. Erin understood now what Mattie meant when she said that they used everything the pig had but the grunt.

Douglas had returned to work, but Erin noticed he stayed well clear of the actual butchering area, concentrating his efforts on salting the meat and setting it in the smokehouse. Meanwhile, all afternoon Tucker brought in tub loads of meat and set them in front of her on the table. Perhaps it was her imagination, but when he brought in the last basin, she thought she saw a small measure of admiration in his eyes.

The men finished their work in the twilight and cleaned up the yard. Mattie put some boiled tongue and liver pudding out with sliced bread for supper so that the men could serve themselves while she finished her work in the kitchen.

Erin couldn't ever remember being so tired. Stray strands of hair clung to her face. Her hands were swollen and nicked from her clumsy work with the knife, and there was a sharp pain between her shoulder blades.

"Only thing left now is to pour off the lard," Mattie said. "You go rest yourself at the table and have some coffee. I'll finish up."

"Mattie, how do you do it? I'm exhausted."

Mattie smiled. "Well, child, first thing you learn about being a country girl is, you always got strength to do what you have to. The Lord won't put no more on your shoulders than you're able to carry."

"Wagon's pullin' in the yard. Looks like Brother Butler,"

called Ben.

"I wonder what he wants," Erin said.

"Pigs' feet. That man's plumb foolish about pigs' feet. I told him we was butchering and he asked me would I save him some feet," said Mattie.

Tucker walked to the back door. "Shame he couldn't show up for some of the work."

Mattie gave Tucker a slap on the arm. "You hush that talk and let him in, Tucker Gillam, or I'll take a switch to you."

Tucker did as he was told and Reverend Butler blustered through the door.

"How do, Tucker, Miz Erin. Miz Mattie! Bless God, it's good to see you! I'm sorry to trouble you on your butchering day, you being so busy and all."

"Not so busy that I forgot your pigs' feet," Mattie said, and she handed him a box packed full.

"Well, bless your heart for thinking of me like that. You'll surely have a crown of glory in heaven, Miz Mattie."

Butler tucked his prize underneath his arm and turned to Erin. "The main reason I come by was to see you, Miz Erin. I've been meaning to come talk to you about Enlo."

"Yes, I apologize for not visiting your home before now to talk to you, but with the funeral and all. . ."

"Ain't no need to apologize. I jist wanted you to know how sorry I was for the ruckus he caused. Enlo's always been hard-headed. But a glorious thing done happened. I was preaching at the Courtois church last week and Enlo got religion! He's sorry for his meanness, and he wants to come back to school, if you'd have him."

"If Enlo is ready to abide by the class rules, he is welcome to return."

"Oh, he'll mind, Miz Erin. I promise you that."

"We will see him Monday then."

Reverend Butler spoke his goodbyes and set his hat back on his head. Douglas came into the kitchen just as he drove away. "So, Enlo has reformed, has he?"

"You heard?" Erin asked. "What do you think?"

"I suppose time will tell, but in the meanwhile, I wouldn't turn your back on him."

"Ain't that kindly a cynical attitude for a Preacher?" Tucker asked.

"I guess maybe it is, Tucker."

thirteen

"Carry your books to school, Miss Corbett?"

"Well, sir, I don't know; folks might talk."

"Let them," Douglas replied. "These people aren't happy unless they have a story about the preacher to tell over their Sunday chicken."

"Come get these books, and don't be so cross," Erin said. "I need to get an early start so I can see what you've done to my school while I was gone."

"Don't worry, everyone survived. Though why you would actually look forward to returning to that crude, chaotic group of children is beyond me."

"I'm afraid the chaos is mostly my fault, but it's a beautiful morning for a new start."

Douglas laughed. "Erin, have you even looked at the sky? It's cold and dull and gray."

Erin stopped in the middle of the road and looked at Douglas. "I'm serious about this," she said. "I intend, by God's grace, to make this school a success."

"All right, Erin, I just don't want you to be hurt if things don't work out."

"I mean to make it work."

Douglas seemed surprised by her determination. "I'm sure you do," he said. "But it would hardly be the end of the world if the school folds. In all the time we've been here, I have yet to persuade these people to listen to a word I say. They haven't budged an inch. I'm not sure they can be reached."

"Of course they can be reached, Douglas. Perhaps you should make some effort to adapt to their ways. . ."

"Don't start that again, Erin. I don't think I'll ever look at another slice of bacon without feeling ill."

They walked up the schoolhouse stairs and went inside. "Let's not quarrel," Erin said. "I didn't mean to upset you."

Douglas put his arm around her waist and pulled her close to him. "I couldn't be upset with you for very long." He kissed her gently and then cupped his hand beneath her chin. "Very well. Do whatever you like. But please try to remember that our term is only for one year. There's no point in getting too attached to these children." He took his watch from his vest pocket. "I must go. I promised to visit Narcissy Hinkle and her new baby this morning. Good luck today, Erin."

The children arrived and scuffled noisily to their seats. Sariah's desk was painfully empty, as was her brother's. Erin wondered if Rabe would ever be allowed to return to school. Just as she closed her roll book, Enlo and Winifred appeared in the doorway.

"Enlo, you and your sister are tardy," Erin said. "We begin school at nine o'clock. Please be sure that you are on time tomorrow."

Enlo took off his hat and stepped forward. "Yes'm. We would've been here, except a big stick of firewood flew up and hit Winifred whilst she was chopping this morning. It took some time for Pa to doctor it up." Enlo stepped aside to reveal the bandage on his sister's arm.

"I see. Are you all right, Winifred, or would you like me to send someone for Dr. Stone?"

Winifred dropped her head and spoke softly. "No'm, Pa done tended it already."

"Please take your seats then."

To her surprise, Enlo obeyed without a word.

"Good morning, class," Erin began. "It is good to be back with you. I hope you were helpful to Reverend Teterbaugh in my absence." Erin stepped in front of her desk. "The past week has been difficult for us all. Sariah was a very special little girl and we'll miss her. We can take comfort in the fact that she is in heaven now, and we can trust that God is taking good care of her."

Erin leaned back on her desk and looked into the children's faces. "I'm afraid that our school has gotten off to a rather bad start. That is mostly my fault. You see, this is my very first school, and I have much to learn about being a teacher. But, starting today, things are going to be different. I would like us all to be friends, but you must understand that from now on, I will not tolerate any nonsense. No more pranks, no more talking out, nor any more horseplay. Anyone who chooses not to follow the rules will be punished. Do you all understand?"

There was a quiet chorus of "yes, ma'ams."

"Good."

❧

The next few weeks brought a virtual transformation in the children. A consistent routine and firm discipline solved most of the behavior problems, and in the process, the children began to show real academic promise. For the first time, Erin felt the pure joy of helping young minds learn.

Several of the children were very bright indeed. Ameriky Reynolds was completing arithmetic assignments almost as fast as Erin could hand them out, and he had a remarkable ability to recall dates. Jackson Witbeck, though only eight, was nearly ready for the fifth reader, and Beulah Stiles could draw beautifully detailed pictures of the animals she saw in the woods.

Of course, not all of the children were as gifted, and Erin wasn't sure what to think about Enlo. He was polite and compliant enough, but there was still something about him that made her uneasy. Erin felt guilty doubting the boy's sincerity, but something about him just didn't ring true.

Winifred was a problem of a different sort. She was a shadow, slipping silently in and out of place. When she spoke, her eyes never left the floor. Her rounded shoulders seemed to carry a burden far too heavy for one so young. Surely there was a way to ease the sadness that enveloped her. Erin determined to pray daily that God would somehow use her to touch the child's life.

One afternoon, snow began to fall a few minutes before the end of the school day. Winter had come to Lost Creek at last. Even the older children couldn't resist peering out the windows as the first flakes floated to the ground.

"The first snow is always special," Erin said. "You may go, but remember to do your homework."

The children grabbed their books and ran out with their faces toward the sky. They danced between the snowflakes, their mouths open wide to catch them on their tongues. Everyone left quickly, except Ben.

"Did you forget something?" Erin asked.

Ben shifted nervously. "No'm. I was jist wondering if you'd have need of someone to rub the board clean."

"All right, Ben. Thank you."

Erin turned in her chair and watched him while he worked. Ben had generally done his best to ignore her and Douglas ever since the barn raising. His willingness to help now puzzled her.

"Thank you for erasing the boards, Ben."

"Ain't nothing, jist thought it needed doing." Ben stopped and stroked at the wool on the eraser. "What changed you, Miz Erin?"

"Changed me? What do you mean?"

"You're different than you was. . .not jist at the school, makin' us mind and all, but other times. You're sort of peaceful-like now. You kindly remind me a little of Mattie."

"That is about the nicest thing you could say to me, Ben." Erin sensed a door was opening in Ben that might never open again. She walked over to the recitation bench. "Come here," she said. He sat down on the bench beside her. "I don't know how else to put it, except that God changed me. I got to a point where I couldn't go one step further on my own. I wanted to give up and go home. Then Mattie showed me that I had to admit how weak I was before God could make me strong. Anything good you see in me is God's doing."

Ben seemed to be considering what Erin had said. "You reckon God would do the same thing for me?"

"Of course He would, Ben, if you ask Him."

"I don't know. I always thought God was mostly out ready to

stomp on folks for their meanness. I reckon I been mad at Him for a long while now."

"That's all right. God's big enough to handle your anger. Just be honest with Him. He loves you more than anything, Ben."

"Would y'show me what to do?"

"It's not difficult. First, you need to tell God you've sinned— you know—done bad things."

"I done plenty of sins, I know that. I feel right bad about it sometimes."

"God gave us a way to get rid of those bad feelings," Erin said. "Imagine if you went home and deliberately broke out the kitchen window. . ."

"Tucker'd have my hide for that."

"I guess he would, and you would deserve it, too. But what if Jube stood between you and Tucker and said, 'I'm taking Ben's licking for him, because I love him.' That's sort of what Jesus did for us when He died on the cross."

"I reckon Jesus must love us a lot."

"He does, Ben, and if we'll ask Him into our hearts, He'll give us that love inside to stay."

Ben frowned. "I don't know as I understand that part about asking Jesus into your heart."

"That's just a figure of speech. It means to be a Christian you have to ask Jesus to be your Savior and Lord. He'll save you from your sins and give you eternal life—and then you have to let Him be in control of your life. Do you want that?"

"Yes'm. I reckon I do."

"You can ask Him right here and now, if you'd like."

Ben bowed his head. He was silent for a long moment, but when he lifted his head, his eyes sparkled. "It really works, don't it, Miz Erin!"

Erin put her arm around him and hugged him tight. "It surely does, Ben."

"I reckon my Ma and Pa would be real happy about this, don't you?"

"From what Mattie has told me of your parents, I think they would be very pleased."

"I wisht I knew how Tuck will take to it. Won't Mattie be happy, though?" Ben thought a moment. "Miz Erin, could we keep this our secret, jist until Sunday? I'll git Tucker to come along to church somehow and I'll go forward at the altar call. It'll be my surprise, and it'll let everyone know all at once."

"All right, Ben, it'll be our secret until Sunday."

❧

There was hardly a dry eye in the church that next Sunday when Ben walked down the aisle. Douglas was so surprised that someone had responded to his message, he nearly forgot to give the benediction. Mattie shouted "Glory!" with tears of joy streaming down her face. Even Jube was making use of his handkerchief. Only Tucker stood stoically among the group surrounding Ben, as the entire congregation came by after the service to give him the right hand of fellowship. When they were done, Douglas shook Ben's hand, too.

"We will have to set up a baptism service when the weather warms up, won't we, Ben?"

Mattie looked at Douglas indignantly. "Foot, Preacher! What's wrong with right now? Ben ain't no warm weather Christian, are you, boy?"

"But it's so cold. There's ice on the creek."

"Ice can be broken, Preacher," Jube said. "I'll be glad to do it for you."

Douglas scanned the room for a possible ally. "Tucker, you're Ben's guardian. I'll not go against your wishes. What do you think?"

Tucker looked at Ben thoughtfully. "I reckon if the boy's decided to git religion, he'd better start out standing up for what he believes."

So Ben was baptized in Lost Creek that very afternoon in the presence of most of the members of the mission church. Jube broke away the ice with an ax while the congregation sang "Amazing Grace." Douglas and Ben waded out waist deep into the creek, then Douglas quickly prayed a blessing and plunged Ben under the icy water. Douglas and Ben wrapped themselves in the blankets Mattie had waiting for them, and Mattie grabbed Ben by the shoulders and kissed him roughly on the cheek.

"I been praying for you since you was birthed," she said. "I know without a shadder of a doubt that God has His hand on your life, boy. He's got something special for you. You heed His call when it comes."

Ben blushed and mumbled something, but Erin could tell he was pleased by Mattie's words. Tucker walked away without comment. He untied the horses and climbed up on the wagon seat. Erin wasn't sure whether Tucker had gone along with this winter baptism out of respect for Ben's decision, or because he wanted to see Douglas waist deep in freezing water, but at least he had not tried to squelch his brother's new found faith.

Tucker drove the horses faster than usual as they headed back to the house, so Douglas and Ben would have to spend no more time than was necessary in their wet clothes. The icy dip seemed to have no ill effect on Ben, but Douglas was sniffling before they even got home. Mattie sent him to bed in the cabin and began boiling beef broth on the stove.

"When that's ready, Mattie, I'll take it over to Douglas, if you'd like," Erin said.

Mattie gave her a wry smile. "All right, child." She put the hot broth in a large bowl and covered it with a dish. "Mind you don't burn yourself, and tell the Preacher if the broth don't work, I'll bring him some of my special tonic."

Erin balanced the bowl in her hands and made her way out the back door, being careful not to slip on the steps. A fine, powdery snow sifted down on her hair and caught in her eyelashes, and the air was clean and cold.

Erin was so intent on getting to the cabin without spilling Douglas' soup, that she nearly walked head-on into Tucker as he came from the barn. His arm steadied her on the slippery path.

"Easy there, or you'll be wearin' what's in that bowl."

"It's broth for Douglas," Erin said. "I was just taking it to him."

"Ben's baptizin' give him a chill, did it?"

"I'm sure he'll be fine. By the way, I wanted to thank you for supporting Ben in his decision."

"I ain't one to stand in another person's way when it comes to religion. Besides, I promised Pa I'd let Ben decide for himself."

"But you think Ben is wrong, don't you?"

"Not wrong exactly, jist green as grass. Takes a few years on a man to make him think clear about such things."

"Meaning you don't believe in what Ben did, or in what we teach at the mission?"

"Meaning I got considerable doubts about it. People who really live by what you all preach are few and far between, Miz Erin."

"That may be true, but it is a poor excuse to disbelieve the Gospel."

Tucker gave an exasperated sigh. "Miz Erin, why don't you save such talk for boys of Ben's age and git that broth into your little preacher friend."

He turned around and stomped back into the barn. Erin walked on to the cabin, puzzled by Tucker's reaction.

Lamplight glowed in the cabin window, but there was no sound of footsteps when Erin knocked on the door. She knocked again, and this time she heard a hushed, "Come in."

Erin cracked the door open and peered inside. "Douglas?"

Across the room, Jube lay on his bunk, snoring so loudly it seemed to vibrate the window glass. Douglas sat up on his bed by the door. "Come in, Erin."

"Are you sure it's all right?"

"I can guarantee you won't bother Jube, and I don't feel up to doing anything improper."

Erin walked in and pulled a chair next to Douglas' bed. "Mattie made you this broth. How do you feel?"

"Like I have been frozen alive. I'll probably catch my death."

Erin felt Douglas's forehead. "You have no fever. You'll feel better after you drink this."

"If I get this kind of attention, I may linger on for several days."

"Thank you, sir, but I'll warn you that I'm not at all patient with invalids. Drink this while it's hot. Mattie said to tell you that she has some tonic ready if the broth doesn't work."

"I hate to think about that." Douglas began spooning up the broth.

"Wasn't it exciting to see our first profession of faith today?"

Douglas put his spoon back in the bowl. "Ben tells me you had more to do with his decision than I."

Erin smiled. "He asked me to keep it a secret until today. He wanted to surprise everyone."

"Ben likes you. He says you're doing a good job with the school, Erin. I'm sorry if I haven't been as interested in your work as I should."

"Douglas, the children are finally learning. They're like little sponges, soaking up everything I say. I never dreamed being a teacher would be this exciting."

Douglas looked at Erin uncertainly. "I hope you will find other roles in life as fulfilling, such as being a minister's wife. You never have given me a final answer to my proposal, you know."

"No, I suppose I haven't."

"I need you, Erin. I need your spirit and your simple faith. Can't you see, we are a perfect complement to one another. Don't you want to share in my ministry?"

Jube grunted and rolled over on his side.

"It isn't that," Erin said quietly. "I've barely gotten started with the school. The children are just beginning to show promise."

Douglas took her hand. "I give you my word, we'll find the school a new teacher. Say yes, Erin. I can't bear waiting for an answer any longer." He pulled away. "Or perhaps I'm a fool to think such a beautiful young lady would care that much for me."

Erin put her hand back into his. "Don't talk so, Douglas. I'm sorry. I know it isn't fair for me to put you off."

"Does that mean you have an answer now?"

"All right, Douglas, my answer is yes. I'll marry you."

The soup bowl slid to the side of the bed as Douglas leaned over to give Erin a kiss. "My dear, you've made me the happiest man on earth."

He reached into the dresser by his bunk. "I was saving this for Christmas, but since it's just two weeks away, I think you should have it now." He opened a small box. "This was my mother's. I'd like you to have it as an engagement ring." He slid the garnet ring on her finger.

"Thank you," was all Erin could say.

"Let's go tell everyone right away," Douglas said.

Erin thought a moment. "Well, yes, I suppose we could, but perhaps it would be better to wait for just a little while. Why don't we tell everyone on Christmas Day?"

"Very well, we'll put the ring back in its box until Christmas, but you keep it in your room. As long as you have it, I feel as if our engagement is official."

The sky was nearly dark by the time Erin left the cabin. The snow had stopped, but it seemed much colder. For some odd reason, the twilight made Erin feel afraid. As she hurried along the path, the snowy yard which had earlier been so calm and clean now seemed eerie and empty.

fourteen

The children's enthusiasm about the school Christmas party made the last few days of the winter term pass quickly. Erin had promised the children a Christmas tree, the first for most of them, with tinsel and candles. This would be a party the children would remember all of their lives. Erin could hardly wait for it to begin.

That morning Mattie was up early cooking a breakfast of fried pork chops and hot applesauce. Douglas ate before everyone else and, as a special favor to Erin, went to the schoolhouse to start the fire and put the finishing touches on the tree. Mattie was setting the platters on the table when Tucker and Jube stomped up on the back porch. They were covered with white from head to toe.

"Mercy!" Mattie cried. "Shake that off outside. I ain't got time to follow you around with a rag."

"Sorry, Mattie," Tucker said. "It's coming down something fierce."

All during the meal, Jube was keeping a watchful eye on the window. "Miz Erin, I best hitch up the mules," he said. "It'll be a slippery walk to school this morning."

"Oh no, Jube, thank you. I love to walk in the snow, and there's only a few inches right now. Besides, Douglas has the cutter at the school already. I can ride home with him."

Tucker frowned and wiped his mouth on his napkin. "If this keeps up, there'll be a foot or more by the time school lets out. That road can git tricky in the drifts, especially with a city boy driving. I'll bring the sleigh for both of you this evening and carry you in."

"I appreciate your concern. But I think Douglas is more than capable of getting us home in the cutter. After all, he grew up driving through the streets of Chicago."

"Well now, that makes all the difference in the world. City

driving will come in handy when the snow gits so high you can't see the sides of the road. Like as not you'll be in a ditch or a drift before you git out of the schoolyard."

Erin folded her napkin and put it on the table. "I assure you that we can manage to find our way home without damage to your cutter or your livestock," she said. "Now, if you will excuse me, it's time I left for school."

"Miz Erin, you are the stubbornest woman I ever laid eyes on," exclaimed Tucker. "When you and that preacher boy bury the cutter, you cut that horse loose. At least he's got sense enough to find his way home."

Erin put on her coat and slammed the door behind her. As she walked down the hill, the snow fell in fluffy clumps so heavy they made soft plopping sounds as they landed. Blankets of white capped even the smallest tree branches with a layer of icing. The muffled calm of the winter forest began nudging away at her angry thoughts.

The program began with fast-paced games called "Snap" and "Winkem," and then, when the children were ready to settle down, Erin taught them how to play "Authors" using the essays they had studied so far in their *McGuffeys*. Next, each child "spoke a piece" that they had written about Christmas. Erin was reminded again how much she had taken for granted, as she repeatedly heard children wishing for a pair of shoes or a few hair ribbons for their Christmas present.

The younger children entertained them by acting out the nativity story as Douglas narrated. Despite the fact that Joseph tripped on the platform and Mary's "donkey" repeatedly threw her from his back, the play was quite a success. After the actors removed their costumes and were given a round of applause, Erin brought out the baskets laden with special holiday treats. Mattie's sweet cider had been heating on the stove with some cinnamon and cloves, and the children drank it as if it were nectar.

It was then that Erin noticed something peculiar about Enlo. He was seated in the back of the room, and for the past hour he had not joined in the class activities. Fearing he might be ill, she went back to see what was wrong. She had only to come within a few feet of him to detect the source of the problem. *Corn liquor!* Apparently he had kept it hidden on his person in some sort of flask.

"Enlo, I am disappointed in you," Erin said. "You were doing so well lately."

"Aw, Teacher, don't be tetchous. I's jist celebratin' a little early is all."

"That kind of celebration isn't allowed here, Enlo. I'm afraid you'll have to go home."

Enlo didn't move. Douglas stood up from his seat by the stove. "Miss Corbett asked you to leave."

Enlo leaned forward in his desk. "You reckon you can make me go, do you, Preacher?"

Over to her left, Erin saw Ben, Ludie Stiles, and Ameriky Reynolds move silently across the room until they stood shoulder to shoulder behind Douglas. By the crestfallen look on Enlo's face, he had seen them too, and realized that he was outnumbered. Enlo got to his feet.

"I don't want to stay at no babies' play party anyhow." He picked up his hat and walked unsteadily out of the door.

"What a shame," said Erin. "I thought perhaps we were reaching him."

"You can't help everyone," said Douglas. "There's no reason to let Enlo spoil the party for everyone else."

"You're right. Class, let's take our seats and we'll begin singing the Christmas carols."

As Erin listened to the children's clear, sweet voices, her heart filled to the brim with the happy spirit of Christmas. She never imagined so much joy could come from such a simple celebration. When the children finished singing their final song, Douglas went to the front of the room and ceremoniously removed the muslin that had been draped over the Christmas tree. Erin lit the candles, being careful that none of the upper branches would be touched by the flames. The children sat silently, their eyes dancing in the candlelight.

"Oh my, Teacher!" exclaimed Noah Keller, "Ain't it the prettiest thing you ever did see?"

Douglas and Erin began passing out the cookies and candy. Then Erin pulled a box out from under her desk and gave each child their pair of mittens.

"It's jist too much to behold," said Mary Stiles. "Thank you, Teacher." She handed Erin a box wrapped in a red handkerchief and tied with string. "It's from all of us," she said. "We wanted you to know it pleasures us that you're our teacher."

The package contained a carefully embroidered sampler with all the students' names on it. "Thank you. This gift will always be special to me. I'm proud to be your teacher, and I'm proud of everyone in this class, too. Now, since the snow is getting so deep, I think perhaps we should all be on our way. Some of you have a long walk home. Have a happy Christmas, and I'll see you in three weeks."

The children left, carrying their booty and shouting "Happy Christmas" over and over. Erin had just begun to clean up, when the door came open and Winifred Butler slipped back inside. She fumbled in her dress pocket, then she rushed toward Erin and pressed a small bundle in her hand. In the next instant, she bolted for the door.

Wrapped inside an old piece of newsprint was a tiny cross carved of wood and a note which said, "Teacher, I think yore real nice. Winifred."

Douglas read the note over Erin's shoulder. "Looks like you've made a friend."

"I hope so. I have a feeling that child needs one."

"We'd better go, too," Douglas said. "The snow is still coming down hard. Can you get things ready in here while I hitch up the horse? I'll bring the cutter around to the front, so you won't have to walk so far in the snow."

Erin blew out all the candles on the Christmas tree and closed the damper on the stove. She had just picked up her coat when she heard footsteps on the back stairs. She wondered what

Douglas had forgotten. She put down her coat and opened the door. It was Enlo.

"What is it, Enlo? I thought I made myself clear. You're to go home."

Enlo lurched into the schoolhouse. Wherever he had been, it was obvious that he had not stopped drinking. He leaned toward Erin until he was just a few inches from her face.

"Now, Teacher," he said. "It's Christmas, and I didn't even git no presents."

Erin gathered his gifts from her desk and held them up to him. "All right, here is the candy and mittens we gave to the rest of the students. Have a happy Christmas, Enlo. Now, I really think you should go on your way."

Enlo smiled. "Thank you, Teacher, but I come to git my real present. I ain't had my Christmas kiss."

The look in Enlo's eyes frightened her. Erin stepped back, trying to put her desk between them, but he grabbed her arm.

"Enlo, you'd better let go of me. Douglas will be back in here any minute."

Enlo pulled her over toward him. "Let the Preacher come," he said. "I'll show him how to treat a lady."

Enlo lunged toward her, and without thinking, Erin slapped him across the face as hard as she could. Anger flashed in his eyes. "Feelin' feisty, are you? I can take care of that, too!"

Enlo pressed Erin's shoulders hard against the blackboard. She heard Douglas at the front door.

"Enlo, let go of her immediately."

Enlo smiled and released his hold on Erin. He turned to Douglas. "I been waiting a long time for this, Preacher. Ain't nobody here to help you now."

The poker from the stove was leaning against the wall in the corner. Erin backed away to try and retrieve it. If only Enlo wouldn't notice her!

"Think about what you're doing, Enlo," Douglas said nervously. "You're only going to get yourself into more trouble. Why don't you go on home like Miss Corbett told you to?"

"You know what, Preacher? I think you're afraid of me, and I'm gonna show Teacher here jist how yeller you are."

Enlo reached into his boot and drew his knife. "Here's how it is, Preacher. You light out of here and I won't put a mark on your pretty face, but you go and try to fight me, and I'm gonna skin your hide jist like a rabbit for Saturday stew. Now, how d'you want it?"

Douglas looked over at Erin. He wavered a moment more and then stepped towards the door. "It seems you leave me no choice."

"Douglas?" Erin watched in disbelief as he opened the door.

"We both know I'm no match for him, Erin. I'll go get help. I'll be back, I promise you."

Enlo laughed. "You do that, Preacher. She might kindly need someone to see her home when I'm through."

"You'd better not harm her, Enlo."

"Or what, Preacher? What you gonna do?" Enlo moved the tip of his knife toward Douglas, and Douglas edged out the door. Enlo laughed and dropped his knife to the floor. He grabbed Douglas by the collar. "Shoot fire, Preacher, I don't even need the knife."

Enlo doubled his fist and hit Douglas square on the jaw, sending him headlong into the door frame. Douglas' body crumpled and he fell to the floor unconscious.

Enlo smiled and walked toward Erin. With her hands behind her back, Erin took a firm hold on the poker and waited until he was within striking distance. Just as he came at her, she swung the poker at him. It hit him hard enough to cause a stream of blood to run down his cheek, but not hard enough to stop him. He wiped his face with the back of his hand.

"Oh, you'll pay for that, Teacher." He tried to pull Erin down to the floor, but she fought to stay upright. He pulled again and she fell sideways onto the stove. The flesh on her left hand seared on the hot metal, but she pushed free, only to have him catch her and throw her down on a desk. He pinned her shoulders, and then his lips were on hers. She tried to turn away, but he pressed his weight on top of her, tearing at the buttons on her shirtwaist.

"Now, don't carry on so, Teacher," he whispered. "I won't hurt you. You're not so high and mighty now, are you, Teacher?"

Erin frantically felt below the desk for anything that she might use as a weapon. Then, for an instant, it was quiet, and in the distance she thought she heard. . .yes, it was. . .sleigh bells! She reached beneath the desk again, grabbed a book, and flung it hard toward the windows. It found its mark and went crashing through the glass.

"Help!" she screamed. "Help me!"

Enlo clamped his hand tightly over her mouth, but Erin heard Tucker's booming voice call to the team and then the sleigh bells jingled furiously. Enlo lost no time making a retreat through the back door.

"Erin?" Tucker was calling to her as he ran up the stairs. "Erin! Where are you?"

She tried to stand, but she couldn't stop shaking long enough to get her balance. Tucker lifted her and helped her into one of the desk seats. "What happened? Are you all right?"

"Yes, I think so. . .it was Enlo." Then, she remembered. "Douglas. . .he's over there. Enlo hurt him."

Tucker looked over to where Douglas lay. He took Erin's coat off the chair where she had left it and wrapped it around her, covering her badly torn shirtwaist, and then he went to Douglas and carefully rolled him over on his back. "He's got a fair-sized knot on his head, but I expect he'll be all right. I best git you two back to the house."

Tucker reached for Erin's hand, but she pulled back in pain. "What's wrong?"

"I burned my hand when I fell against the stove."

Tucker gently took her hand in his and pulled away the scorched sleeve. "That's a bad burn," he said. "It's already blistered up."

"Funny, it doesn't hurt very much."

"It will. You set here with the Preacher while I unhitch the horse from the cutter."

Tucker tied the horse to the rear of the big sleigh, then he came back into the school. He carried Douglas out and covered him with a lap robe. Finally, he came in for Erin.

"Would you be more comfortable in the back with the Preacher, or would you ruther ride on the seat?"

"If you don't mind, I think I would rather ride up front with you."

Tucker put his arm around her waist. "You jist hang on to me," he said. "I'll have you home in no time."

ża

There was a flurry of activity when they arrived at the house. Tucker carried Douglas into Erin's bedroom, since Mattie's bed was not long enough for a full grown man. Jube went for Dr. Stone, and Mattie guided Erin to a chair by the fireplace. At first, Erin felt as if she were a spectator to everything that happened around her, but a cup of strong tea and the warm quilt Mattie wrapped around her shoulders brought her to her wits. Mattie sat down next to Erin with a plate of salted butter and began doctoring her hand. Tucker was right; it had begun to hurt.

"How is Douglas?" Erin asked.

"He don't seem too bad hurt to me. Tucker'll stay with him till Doc gits here." Mattie pushed the hair back that had fallen around Erin's shoulders. "You hurt anywhere else, child? You know you can tell ole Mattie if that boy. . ."

"No, Mattie, nothing except a few blisters and bruises."

The back door opened, and Jube hustled Dr. Stone in.

"Glory, Doc, how'd you git here so fast?" Mattie asked.

"Jube found me at Widder Puckett's. Her bursitis is acting up again."

As the doctor went in to examine Douglas, Tucker came out and unlocked the gun cabinet in the front hall. He and Jube each took a shotgun and a handful of cartridges. Tucker wore a grim look that Erin had never seen before.

"You'll be going right out, I reckon," Mattie said.

Tucker nodded. "Ain't no telling if the snow might start up again and wipe out the tracks by morning."

There was concern in Tucker's eyes when he looked at Erin. "Mattie, you have the Doc check on Miz Erin when he gits done with the Preacher," he said. "From the looks of the schoolhouse, Enlo got pretty rough."

The shotguns frightened Erin. "Enlo wouldn't have done it if he had been sober," she said. "He's only a boy, really."

"Being young and drunk don't excuse it," Tucker said firmly.

"Don't fret, Miz Erin," Jube said. "We don't aim to use these 'lest Enlo don't give us no choice."

"That old couch ain't fit to sleep on," said Tucker. "You bed Miz Erin down in my room tonight, Mattie. If we git back before morning, I'll bunk out with Jube. Tell Ben to look after things while we're gone."

"Wait a minute," Mattie said. She took a woolen scarf off the peg by the door and wrapped it around Jube's neck. "There, you old fool. I reckon I got enough to do 'round here without you coming down with the grip."

"Don't wait up," said Tucker, and then they were gone.

After Dr. Stone checked Erin over, Mattie got a nightgown and wrapper from her room and they went upstairs. Erin had seldom been on the upper floor of the house, and it felt strange now to be in Tucker's room.

The day and Dr. Stone's pain medicine were taking their toll. By the time Erin changed into her nightclothes, she dropped gratefully into the soft feather bed and went to sleep.

When Erin awoke the next morning, it was already light enough for her to see Tucker's room. There was a sense of order here, like one might expect in a banker's room, but certainly not a farmer's. A massive secretary desk dominated the south wall. Its shelves were filled with books.

Erin slipped out of bed and walked over for a closer look. A title caught her eye, *The Harmony of the Gospels*. She had seen some of the same texts on Douglas' shelves in the cabin. Erin opened the cabinet and took out a Bible commentary from the bottom shelf. There was an inscription on the inside of the cover: "Always put God first. Love, Pa and Ma, May 1877."

This was a pastor's library. Why would Tucker have these books in his room? They didn't look as if they had been touched for quite some time. She saw something sticking out of a concordance on the top shelf, and she took the book down and carefully pulled the paper out. It was a Certificate of Ordination, dated July of 1878, and it had Tucker's name on it. Tucker was an ordained minister!

While Erin was considering her discovery, she heard the clank of milk pails outside in the yard. Breakfast must be almost ready. She quickly returned the book and put on her wrapper.

Mattie was busy at the stove frying eggs when Erin came down. Ben had the milk on the porch and was filling the milk cans. The empty pails dropped with a loud bang, and he raced through the door.

"Mattie! Tucker and Jube are back. They're coming up the road right now!"

"Fine, boy, ain't no need to git so flustered. They know their way in. Go take your coat off and set down to the table."

Tucker and Jube came in the house and went straight for the coffeepot. Tucker rubbed his hands together over the stove. Erin couldn't stand not knowing. "Tucker, did you find Enlo?"

Tucker sighed. "No, Miz Erin. We tracked him back to his Pa's cabin, but he'd already lit out of there, too."

Tucker and Jube exchanged looks.

"What's wrong, Tuck?" Mattie asked.

"We found Silas Butler in his cabin. He's dead."

fifteen

"What about Winifred? Where is she?"

"I don't know, Miz Erin. Wasn't no sign of the girl nor Enlo. We found Butler on the floor, shot in the chest. These tags were laying to the side." Tucker scattered half a dozen ear tags on the table.

"Those are from our cattle!" Mattie exclaimed. "Land sakes, I knew Enlo was a dilatory sort of boy, but I never thought him to be a murderer and a rustler to boot!"

"We have to find Winifred," Erin said. "If Enlo would kill his own father, there's no telling what he would do to her."

"I know. Soon as Jube and I can get a bite to eat, we'll go round up some men to hunt for them." Tucker looked toward the dining room. "Ben, you might as well come around from that door. I know you're there."

Ben stepped sheepishly into the kitchen.

"You reckon you can ride over to Berryman and have Mr. Doss send word to the sheriff at Potosi what's happened?" Tucker asked.

Ben stood up straight. "Yes, sir, Tucker, I'll go right now."

"You won't either," Mattie said. "Not before you eat some breakfast."

"I ain't hungry, Mattie, honest."

"Mattie's right," Tucker said. "Another half hour more or less won't matter now. It's too cold a ride for an empty belly."

Fatigue showed around the men's eyes, but they filled their plates quickly, eager to get back out and search for Winifred.

"How's the Preacher?" Tucker asked.

"Good enough to set up and take a meal," Mattie said. "I believe he can move back to the cabin tonight."

Jube and Tucker set out again to find Winifred, and Ben left on horseback for Berryman. Mattie and Erin were left in the quiet of the morning with the breakfast dishes.

"Do you think Winifred is all right?" Erin asked.

"I don't know, child, but there's a bigger Hand that's workin' in this. Let Him simmer on it a while."

"Mattie, you really believe God has a plan for everything that happens in our lives, don't you?"

"Well, surely the Good Book says so."

Erin realized she was still wiping a dish that was long past dry, and she reached for another.

"What troubles you, child?" Mattie asked.

"Do you think God has one special person picked out for us to marry?"

"Well, I reckon God always has His best planned out for us, if we're willin' to see it. You believe you found that person, do you?"

Erin put the dish up on the shelf. "I thought perhaps I had, but now I'm not so certain."

Mattie spread a fresh cloth over the kitchen table. "It's been a tiresome day or two—ain't no time to be deciding for sure on such things. But you mind this, don't never marry a man who ain't a friend first, and don't settle for someone who has less a heart for God than you do. No matter how pretty the package, you won't be happy."

Erin spent the rest of the day thinking about what Mattie had said. She couldn't deny she was deeply hurt by Douglas' attempted desertion at the schoolhouse, but to give up on the plans they had made seemed awfully harsh.

I'm being silly, she thought. *Douglas loves me. This will all work out in time.*

≈

Tucker and Jube finally came home late that night. Tucker pulled a chair up close to the hearth and struggled to take off his boots. He looked exhausted.

"I think the coffee is still hot," Erin said quietly. "Mattie banked the fire in the stove before she went to bed."

"You're a little old to wait up for Santy Claus, ain't you?"

Erin had forgotten this was Christmas Eve. She watched

Tucker hold his stiff fingers in front of the fire.

"There's a beef roast in there too, if you're hungry."

"We had a bite at the Kellers', but some hot coffee would go real nice."

Erin went to the kitchen and poured him a steaming cup. "I'm afraid it's very strong."

"Long as it's hot. I'm about frozen." Tucker took the cup and sipped loudly. "That is stout, but it hits the spot."

"Did you find anything?"

Tucker shook his head. "We walked the better part of twenty miles, but there was no sign of Enlo or Winifred. The wind had blown over most all the tracks."

"I guess there isn't anything more we can do, is there, except to pray. Winifred was just beginning to open up to me at school."

"She is a quiet little thing." Tucker looked at the bandage on Erin's hand. "Is that hurting you?"

"Oh, no, not really. It just throbs a bit if I don't keep it propped up."

They watched the orange and yellow flames dance among the logs. The warm firelight illuminated Tucker's face as he poked at a piece of wood that had fallen on the hearth. Erin thought it odd that she had found him so unattractive when they'd first met. In his own rugged way, she decided, he was almost handsome.

"Tucker, why did you come after Douglas and me yesterday, after I told you not to?"

Tucker grinned. "Could be I'm the only one around here who can out-stubborn you."

"You might be right. Anyway, I am glad you came when you did. I don't think I thanked you."

"No thanks needed," he said. "But you're welcome. While I think on it, there's something I want you to have, kindly a little Christmas present. I best give it to you now, because I jist might sleep through part of Christmas."

Tucker reached up and took a small green box down from

the mantle. He handed it to Erin. She opened the box and found a delicate cameo pin.

"It's beautiful."

"I know it ain't much for a city gal like you, but you're doing a good job at the school, and you took the grieving out of Ben. I wanted you t'know I'm grateful."

"I'll treasure it, Tucker, thank you."

"You're welcome." He yawned. "I'm bone tired. I believe I'll go on up to bed. Merry Christmas, Miz Erin."

"Merry Christmas, Tucker."

❧

Christmas morning dawned cold and bright. Delicious smells penetrated Erin's room, so she dressed quickly in the cold and went to the kitchen.

Mattie had outdone herself for Christmas breakfast. Chicken was frying on the stove, ham and eggs were in the warmer, and the oven was full of yeasty sweet rolls. Presents sat stacked on each chair, ready for opening. Erin hurriedly added her gifts to the piles. Ben passed by her at the kitchen door with silverware in his hands.

"Good morning, Ben."

"Happy Christmas, Miz Erin."

"I see I've been replaced," Erin said to Mattie in the kitchen.

Mattie laughed. "I thought the boy might be too growed up for Christmas this year, but he was up before the chickens, trying to hurry things along so's he could open his presents."

At Mattie's summons, everyone assembled for breakfast. Tucker was there despite his prediction that he might sleep in. Douglas came in looking pale but otherwise recovered.

"May I talk with you later?" he whispered to Erin. "Perhaps in the barn after breakfast?"

"All right."

Douglas slipped by her to his seat. Ben wolfed down every bite of his breakfast and sat waiting impatiently while everyone else finished. Tucker laughed aloud at him.

"Boy, I ain't never seen such a case of all over fidgets," he said. "Go on, git to your presents before you bust."

Ben grabbed for his packages. There was a new shirt from Mattie, a copy of *Pilgrim's Progress* from Douglas and Erin, and a prized slingshot from Jube. The last present was from Tucker. It was a Bible. Ben carefully turned the pages.

"It's Ma's, ain't it, Tucker?"

"I reckon she'd want you t'have it now. Mind, you take care of it."

"I will, Tucker, thanks."

Brown paper piled up high on the table as the presents were opened. Erin came to Douglas' gift and lifted the lid of a velvet jewel case. Inside, on a red lining, were a pair of stunning gold earrings with diamond centers, and a brooch to match. Douglas looked at her expectantly.

"They are beautiful, Douglas, but it's too much."

"Nonsense. I had my father send them from Chicago. A beautiful lady deserves beautiful things. Here, put them on so I can see how lovely you look."

Douglas' voice seemed just a trifle too loud as he removed Tucker's cameo from Erin's collar and pinned on his brooch. Erin's cheeks flushed. She glanced up and saw that Tucker was watching her carefully. He frowned and Erin looked away. She picked up Tucker's brooch and put it in her pocket.

She took a load of dishes into the kitchen and put them in a pan full of hot soapy water. What was she going to do about Douglas? His gift was lovely, but she could not get the scene at the schoolhouse out of her mind. Still, she had no reason to care if Tucker Gillam was disappointed in her. She owed him no explanations.

Mattie looked over her shoulder. "Erin Corbett, I told you not to git that hand wet. Now git out of that dishwater."

"I'm sorry, I forgot. There's so much to do for dinner, I was just trying to help."

Mattie sighed, but her eyes smiled. "Won't help none if you git the sickness from blood pizen. Go set at the table and I'll put on a dry bandage."

Erin sat down obediently while Mattie removed the wet dressing. "Mattie, would you answer a question for me?"

"If I can, child."

"Well, that night I slept in Tucker's room, I noticed all the books he has. . .and I saw his ordination certificate."

"You must'a done some powerful hard noticing."

"I suppose I was being nosy, but I can't help wondering. . . why did Tucker leave the ministry?"

Mattie thought for a moment. "I reckon he wouldn't have sent you up there if he cared that you saw them things."

"You think he wanted me to see them?"

Mattie nodded. "I don't expect he'd own up to it, though, even to hisself."

"Why did he quit the ministry, Mattie?"

"Oh, 'twas more than one thing, really. Mostly, it was a little gal named Laurie, prettiest thing you ever seen, but that's kindly jumpin' ahead of the story."

She sighed. "See, Tucker got his start in the ministry from a preacher who settled in here jist after the war. Brother Roberts was a big man with friendly ways. I reckon that's why Tucker took to him so. They'd oft times burn lamplight together and Brother Roberts would teach Tucker what he learned when he was at Bible college. Tucker's Ma and Pa had one of their proudest days when Tucker got ordained to preach.

"Tucker took a church a half day's ride north of here, and was doing right well. That's when Laurie and her parents moved into the valley and joined his congregation. Tucker fell plumb foolish in love with her, and they was fixing to take the world by its ears."

"They were going to marry?" asked Erin.

"Oh yes, jist as soon as all the particulars could git arranged. Laurie's family hailed from Kansas City, and her grandaddy helped Tucker git called to a city church up there somewheres. Laurie was tickled pink that she was going to get out of these sticks and go back to where she was raised."

"So she and Tucker moved to Kansas City?"

"No. It didn't work out that way. Before they could git hitched, Brother Roberts was killed sudden like from a fall off his horse, and Tucker felt the call to come back here and pastor where he growed up.

"At first, Laurie went along with the idea, but after she took a hard look at the kind of life she was bound to have here, she told Tucker he'd have to choose between her and his country church. Tucker stood his ground, and as far as I know, he never heard from her again. Word had it that she run off with a dry goods drummer not six weeks later."

Mattie shook her head. "Long about then, Tucker's ma took bad sick. She had the consumption and she suffered something terrible at the end. Seems like Tucker took his hurt about Laurie and Brother Roberts and his ma out on the Lord. He allowed as he jist couldn't confidence a God who'd let his sweet mama suffer so. Didn't help that the woman who'd promised to work shoulder to shoulder with him turned her back at the first sight of plain living. He locked his preachin' books up and buried hisself with farm work, helping his daddy. It bittered him and now it's like he's got a hard spot on his heart when it comes to religion."

"I think I understand how he felt. . .I mean, well, it's hard when people don't live up to our expectations, especially those given to the ministry."

"We're all walking the same path, child, even those called to preach," Mattie said. "Some jist ain't as far on their journey as others. That's why we got to keep looking to the Master as our guide, instead of the folks on the road around us."

"At least I understand why Tucker was so skeptical when we first came to Lost Creek," Erin said. "He told me I would turn and run home when I saw what kind of job this was going to be."

"Ain't no finer man in these hills than Tucker Gillam. It's jist that he and his Creator got things that ain't settled atwixt each other."

Erin went to collect the men's coffee cups from the parlor.

Through the dining room window, she saw Douglas going into the barn. She had forgotten about her promise to meet him after breakfast. She took the cups into the kitchen and got her coat.

The wind in the yard was bitter cold. Erin was glad to reach the relative warmth of the barn, but just as she got to the door, she heard loud, angry voices from inside.

"You mean to tell me you was leaving her alone with Enlo?" Tucker asked.

"If you will put me down, my good man, I will try to explain," Douglas replied angrily.

"Don't tempt me, Preacher. If I put you down right now, I'll do the job proper."

Erin rushed in the door. Tucker had Douglas pinned up against the wall, his feet dangling above the dirt floor.

"Tucker, stop it this instant!" Erin demanded. "Let him go!"

Tucker set Douglas down on his feet and stepped back. "I thought the Preacher got hurt trying to look after you. Why didn't you tell me this namby was leaving you to fight off Enlo by yourself?"

"Perhaps I thought it was none of your business. Douglas and I haven't even had a chance to discuss it yet. Besides, brute force isn't the answer to everything, you know."

Tucker picked up his hat from the floor and brushed it clean, then he shook his head. "Well, aren't you two a pair." He gave Douglas a disgusted look and walked out the barn door.

"Thank you for standing up for me, darling," Douglas said. "I wasn't sure you understood."

"I'm not sure I do."

"Erin, you don't think I intended to leave you with Enlo, do you? I would have come back. . .you do believe that, don't you?"

Tucker's big chestnut mare whinnied from her stall. Erin went over to her and stroked the horse's neck. "I'm not sure what to believe, Douglas. Perhaps I have judged you too harshly."

Douglas took her hand. "Don't make this a stumbling block between us," he pleaded. "I'm sorry you're upset, but when we get back to the city, this dreadful incident won't matter any more. I'll make it up to you, I promise I will. Now, give me your pretty smile and say it's all right."

"It isn't that simple, Douglas. . ."

Douglas drew Erin close and pressed her head on his shoulder. "We're not in the same class as these people, Erin. We weren't bred to deal with their violence and their base way of life. Our assignment is nearly half way through, and then I promise I'm going to see to it that you have everything you've ever done without."

"You sound as if you simply intend to mark time here until our term is finished," Erin said. "There is so much to be done here, Douglas. Don't you think God called us here for a reason?"

Douglas leaned back against a post and inspected his fingernails. "I'm not sure what you mean by 'God calling us here,' Erin. I'm here because my father insisted I get practical experience in the ministry before he would help me get a position in a good church."

Douglas saw the disappointment in Erin's eyes. "Erin, you're overwrought, and who could blame you after the ordeal you've endured. This isn't the time to discuss theology. Kiss me, and then let's go in and have a cup of tea. We can talk about this later. I'm nearly frozen."

Erin turned away. "No, Douglas, you go on ahead."

"Very well, I'll be in the cabin should you change your mind." He buttoned his coat over his chest and stormed out across the yard. Erin leaned her face against the mare. Douglas seemed to be slipping farther and farther away.

❧

The day after Christmas, Erin sat at the breakfast table feeling grumpy and out of sorts.

"What ails you, child? You hardly touched your food."

"It's nothing, Mattie. I'm just not particularly hungry this morning."

Mattie sniffed and carried the last dish into the kitchen. She always took it personally when someone didn't eat one of her meals.

After they finished the dishes, Mattie began to pack a small wooden crate full of medical supplies. Tucker stopped short on a trip to the barn when he saw what she was doing.

"Is Rose Stiles fixing to have her baby, Mattie?"

"Could be anytime now. I thought I'd take these things on over to the house today. Least ways, they'll have what they need if her time comes before I can git there. It'll be that much less I have to tote along when I'm in a hurry."

As Tucker started toward the door, they heard a soft tapping sound at the front of the house.

"I believe that's someone knocking on the front door," Mattie said.

Tucker opened the door, and there on the porch stood Winifred Butler! Mattie hurried to the forlorn little figure. "Are you all right, child? Come set by the fire and git warm." She led Winifred over to Tucker's big arm chair and wrapped her in a quilt.

"Did your brother hurt you, honey?" Tucker asked. "Do you know where Enlo is?"

Winifred shook her head. "No sir, I ain't seen him. I come here for something else. I come to turn myself in to the sheriff and git arrested."

"You?" Erin said. "What could you have done that the sheriff would want to arrest you?"

Winifred's eyes filled with tears and she looked down at the floor. "It was me who kilt Pa."

Tucker bent down in front of her. "Now you look at me, Winifred, and you tell me the truth. Did Enlo make you come here and say that?"

"No, sir. I'm tellin' the honest truth. I ain't seen Enlo since the night...the night Pa died. I'm ready to go to jail for what I done, Mr. Gillam. It don't matter what happens to me anyway."

"Of course it matters," Erin said.

Tucker pulled the quilt over Winifred's trembling arms. "Winifred, supposin' you start at the beginning and tell us how all this come about."

"First off," Winifred began, "there's some things about my Pa that folks around here don't know. Preachin' wasn't his only way to make a living."

"Many ministers have other jobs besides preaching," Erin said. "What else did your father do?"

"I'm real sorry, Mr. Gillam, but Pa was the one who butchered your cattle. It started out that Pa'd only take a chicken or two when we was hungry, but then he got to where he would sell the meat at the places he preached. Nobody seemed to mind him selling meat on the side. They figured he raised it his own self."

"Our tags were by your Pa when we found him," Tucker said.

Winifred nodded. "Pa was real perturbed about them. He'd told Enlo to bury all that truck, but I reckon Enlo kept 'em for play pretties. Pa was fixing to strap Enlo for it."

"Then Enlo was involved in the stealing," Erin said.

"Yes'm. Pa's had Enlo working with him for five or six years now. I used to have a sorry feeling for Enlo, especially when Pa whupped him, until I figured out Enlo liked his job of work. Pa sent Enlo to school so's he could keep an eye on things and know 'bout folks' comings and goings. When Enlo got sent home for fighting with Ben, Pa beat the whey outta him. That's why Enlo come back and behaved hisself, least until he found that Christmas whiskey."

Erin could scarcely believe that this was the child who had barely spoken ten words at school. A dam seemed to have broken, and the pent-up words kept tumbling out.

"What happened the night of the school party?" Tucker asked.

"Pa was fit to be tied when he found them ear tags. Said he was gonna teach Enlo to do such a stupid thing. Then Enlo come in gabblin' on about how he'd kilt the Preacher and that you had caught him fooling with Miz Corbett. Pa took out his razor strap and layed into Enlo, calling him shiftless and low down and such, till finally he wore hisself out. Pa thought on it awhile and said he reckoned we'd better move on. We've never stayed no where more'n a few months. Pa told Enlo to light out for his brother's place down in Reynolds County, and he put Enlo out the door right then and there. After that, I started packing things up, while Pa got to drinking. The more he drank, the madder he got at Enlo for making us move in the dead of winter. Enlo wasn't there no more, so Pa come after me."

Tears were pouring down Winifred's cheeks. "I couldn't take no more, Mr. Gillam. I didn't want no more beatings. He done other things, too. . .things pas ought not to do. Whenever he got drunk like that, he'd come after me."

Erin thought of the cuts and bruises Winifred had come to school with and wished now that she had paid them more heed.

"What happened when your pa came after you with his strap?" Tucker asked.

"I told him if he touched me again, I was gonna run off and tell what he done, but he jist got madder and come at me anyway. I ran out the door and I reckon when I slammed it shut, Pa's shotgun fell off the pegs. I heared it fire, and when I looked back inside, . . .Pa was laying on the floor, and he weren't breathing."

Winifred wiped the tears from her face with her palms. "I'm ready to take whatever's due me for what I done."

"Winifred, listen, honey," Tucker said. "Ain't nobody gonna do nothing to you, don't you worry bout that. I promise that I'm gonna see to it that you git taken care of proper from now on."

sixteen

Erin opened the oven and held her hand inside as she had seen Mattie do. The oven felt hot enough for the cornbread, she supposed, so she set the pan in and shut the door.

Tucker came in from his morning chores and looked around the kitchen. "Where's Mattie?"

"Gone to the Stiles'. Emmit came by for her just after breakfast. Mattie said she thought it would be a while yet, since it's Rose's first baby, but she went on anyway. Poor Emmit was beside himself with worry."

Tucker poured a cup of coffee and looked in the pot of beans bubbling on the stove. "You fixing dinner?"

"Yes, I am. It may not be as good as Mattie's, but there's plenty of it. Sit down and I'll fill your plate."

"Ain't that something. I never thought I'd see the day you could turn out a respectable meal on your own."

"I had a good teacher. It looks like you may have to live off my cooking for awhile. Since Rose's mother still has children at home, Mattie thought it would be easier if she stayed and took care of Rose herself during Rose's lying in time, especially since school is out and I can take over here."

Tucker sat down at the kitchen table. "I expect we'll manage. Did the Preacher and Jube get off to Berryman all right?"

Erin hesitated. Tucker was not going to like this piece of news. "Well, Jube left about an hour ago, but Douglas didn't go with him."

"Why not?"

"He had another one of those headaches. It came on all of a sudden. I think he ought to see a doctor. Sometimes head injuries can cause problems for years afterwards."

"The only problem the Preacher had was when he figured out how many drifts they'd have to break to git to Berryman." Tucker got up and reached for his coat. "I best go see if I can

153

catch up with Jube. That old man's got no business shoveling out snow drifts by himself."

"Oh, he didn't go alone. Ben went with him. He promised to shovel all the snow."

Tucker looked uncertain, but he draped his coat over the chair and sat back down. "I reckon Ben is big enough to do a man's job of work. When I was his age, Pa and me was splittin' the chores pretty much down the middle. I forgit the boy is 'most nearly grown." Tucker picked up his fork and began to eat. "Maybe I should've had Jube wait for some of this snow to melt, but I wanted to git word to the sheriff about what happened with Winifred and Reverend Butler. Still, it ain't that far to Berryman, and the cutter is light enough to skim over most of the drifts. Sure was a storm we had. I ain't never seen the like of it."

Erin looked out the kitchen window. The ice that had come with the storm two nights before still covered every tree branch. Sunlight sparkled off the crystal casements with blinding beauty. Nearly two feet of new-fallen snow blanketed the yard.

Her attention was diverted by the smell of something burning. Her cornbread! Erin hurried over to the oven. Fortunately, the cornbread was only brown around the edges. She reached in to retrieve it, but her bandaged hand wouldn't bear the weight of the pan, and it was too heavy to lift out one-handed. Tucker saw her predicament and jumped up to help her.

"Your hand still hurting you?"

"It seemed to be healing," Erin said. "But this morning some of the blisters broke open, and it's a little sore."

Tucker gingerly touched the bandage. "I can feel heat. You best let me have a look."

"Don't be a goose. I've spent the last two hours over the stove. Both of my hands are hot. Now, go finish your dinner." She poured Tucker another cup of coffee. "Do you think Winifred is happy at Widow Puckett's?" she asked.

"Two days is a little too soon to tell, ain't it? She seemed happy enough when I walked over to check on them yesterday.

The Widder and Winifred was busy cutting down some of Bessie's old dresses to size. Winifred looked like she'd struck gold. I doubt she's ever had more'n two dresses at one time."

"I'm glad. I hope the Widow will be kind to her."

"Don't fret about that. The Widder has a tongue sharp enough to cut whetstone, but she's got a good heart. She wouldn't let on, but she's twice as happy to have a youngun in the house again as Winifred is to be there."

Erin lifted the butter out of the window box and set it on the table. "Tucker, does it bother you that Reverend Butler was, well, a charlatan? I mean, I know you have your reasons, but you seem to have a skeptical attitude toward the church. I hope you don't think we're all in the Lord's work for selfish gain."

Tucker sipped his coffee and chuckled. "I was wondering when you'd git around to this. Mattie told me you asked her about the books up in my room. Miz Erin, I reckon that's a subject best left closed between us." His tone of voice was pleasant, but it was clear by the firm set of his jaw that he meant what he said.

"I'm sorry if it seemed I was prying," said Erin. "I'm going to take a plate over to Douglas. There's more food on the stove, if you want it."

Tucker smiled mischievously. "I'd forgotten all about the Preacher. Now, he's one of them unselfish reasons you come to Lost Crick for, ain't he?"

Erin put her shawl around her shoulders and went outside, shutting the door firmly behind her.

❧

Tucker was splitting wood in the sideyard when Erin started back to the kitchen. "How's your Preacher?" he asked.

"Asleep. Now, if you'll excuse me, I have work to do."

Tucker took off his hat and bowed in her direction. She had just reached the house when she thought she heard someone calling.

"Did you hear that?" Erin asked. "It sounded like Ben."

She was right. Ben trotted over the rise and down the hill

toward the house. Tucker and Erin ran to meet him.

"What's wrong, boy?" Tucker asked. "Where's Jube? Is he all right?"

"Jube's all right," Ben said breathlessly. "He sent me here for you and Mattie. It's the Kellers. Their cabin roof is caving in with the weight of all this snow. Mr. Keller waved us down when we went by his place. He's trying to shore up the rafters before the whole thing falls, but it's heavy work. Miz Keller already hurt her back trying to help. Mr. Keller didn't want Jube to try it, so they said I should come git you. They want Mattie to come too, if she can, to help look after the younguns. Miz Keller's abed, and those two boys of hers are giving her fits."

"Mattie's not here, Ben," said Erin. "She went to deliver Rose Stile's baby."

"You want me to go after someone else, Tucker?"

"No, you git in the house and warm up. I'll hitch up the sled and go see what I can do."

"I'll get my coat," said Erin. "I'm going with you."

"No, you ain't. I'll have to take the back road over the river to git the big sled through to the Keller's in all this snow. It's a long, cold ride. You stay here and look after Ben."

"Ben can look after himself," Erin said. "Besides, Douglas is in the cabin."

"You ain't used to this kind of weather. You'd be frostbit before we left the yard. Once we git the roof fixed, I'll take those younguns over to the Witbecks' if Becky's that bad off."

"There's no reason to take those children out in this weather and crowd the Witbecks' little cabin when I can go with you. If Becky's hurt, she'll need a woman to look after her. Now, either you let me ride with you, or I'll walk the hill road through Gobbler's Knob like Ben did."

Tucker took off his hat and ran his hand through his hair. "All right. Go inside and git that medicine bag Mattie keeps in the kitchen, jist in case Becky's in need of some doctorin'. And you git a scarf for your own self, and some mittens. Be back here in five minutes or I'll sure leave you standing."

Erin hurried into the kitchen and looked underneath the table for Mattie's bag. The room tilted dizzily when she stood up. Thankfully, when she took a few deep breaths, her vision gradually cleared. Tucker would never let her hear the end of it if he knew she was lightheaded from a few hours' work in the kitchen. Well, there was no need to let on and give him the satisfaction.

Tucker already had the horses hitched and was waiting in the yard. He took the carpet bag and set it in the back of the sleigh, then he helped Erin up on the seat. Tucker spoke to the horses and the sled began to glide smoothly across the snow.

The bells on the horses' harnesses jingled merrily, as if there were no urgency to the trip at all. But thick gray clouds were moving in over the sun, and the wind began to blow in cold bursts. The icy branches rattled and bumped against one another, and pieces of ice broke off and fell into the snow with muffled thuds. The temperature was dropping, and Erin guiltily realized she had forgotten both the mittens and scarf Tucker had ordered her to bring along. She pulled her hood further down on her head and shoved her hands deep into her coat pockets.

The road was completely obliterated by the heavy snow. Though she had traveled through here many times, Erin had no idea where the side of the road ended and the woods began. A few inches either way meant the difference between traveling on and plunging into a snowy ditch. Twice, the horses floundered, and Tucker had to go in after them, unhitch, pack the snow with his boots, and lead the team out of the drift. Finally, he would rehitch them, and they would be on their way again.

They seemed to be crawling at a snail's pace as the horses struggled in snow up to their withers. The wet cold seeped deeper through Erin's woolen coat, and she began to shiver, even though she tried hard to sit still. Tucker reached in back of the seat and pulled up an old horse blanket.

"Drape this over your shoulders," he said. "Maybe next time you'll listen."

Erin gratefully took the blanket and pulled it around her. "How much longer until we get to the bridge?" she asked.

"Not long, if we don't git stuck in any more drifts."

Tucker tried to turn his coat collar up around his ears, but he couldn't do it with one hand on the reins. Erin reached over and pulled it up for him. Tucker looked at her for a moment, and then went back to driving the team.

"I'm sorry I make you so angry," Erin said. "I'd like you to understand why I insisted on coming along, but I'm not sure how to explain it to you. It's just that I want the people here to be my people now, too. I care about them very much."

For an instant, Tucker looked as if he wanted to believe her, then just as quickly, his eyes grew cold. "So, we're your people now, are we? Maybe till come spring, when the Preacher gives you a better offer. You don't let people into your heart for a time, then jist set 'em aside when something fancier comes along. You been here five months. You ain't even begun to know what really caring for these people is."

"Couldn't I care about the people here and about Douglas, too? And did it ever occur to you that city people need churches and ministers?"

"Of course they do, but that ain't what the Preacher is about, and you'd know that were you jist honest with yourself. That Preacher won't never be anywhere but at some high-toned church where he can have fine clothes and eat supper with society folks. That's why the Preacher wants you. He needs a pretty wife who can entertain his guests and charm the deacons and look grand on his arm by the church door on Sunday morning. You'll git a square deal though—fancy dresses, a big ole house, maybe even a servant or two. If that's what you want, fine and dandy, but don't go talking to me about your calling to the people here at Lost Crick."

"How dare you! By what right do you think you can talk to me like that? You're in no position to evaluate anyone's ministry. You abandoned the ministry!"

Tucker stared at the road up ahead. The bridge was just a few yards away. "You're right," he said. "I did leave the ministry. So, I reckon you and me'll have something in common when you go to marry that Preacher."

"Tucker Gillam, you are the most infuriating man I have ever met, if I. . ." Suddenly, the countryside spun dizzily out of control. Erin grabbed for the side of the sled and held on. Tucker stopped the horses.

"Miz Erin? What's wrong?"

The trees and ground were returning to their rightful places, but the dizzy spell left Erin weak. Her hand was throbbing.

"It's nothing. Haven't you seen a woman swoon before? We spoiled city girls are taught how to do it at an early age. Let's get going."

Tucker put his hand under Erin's chin and turned her face toward him. "Look at you. You're pale as milk, shivering and sweating at the same time. I'm gonna take you back to the house." He picked up the reins and started to back the horses away from the bridge.

"No, you won't! We're halfway there, and the Kellers need our help. Now, you drive those horses across that bridge and no nonsense!"

"That ain't for you to decide."

Erin realized that once they crossed the bridge it would be nearly impossible to turn the horses on the narrow road until they were almost to the Keller farm. On impulse, she grabbed at the reins and urged the team on. The horses pranced nervously, but Tucker regained control.

"What in thunder do you think you're doing? Are you trying to git us killed?" He grabbed her wrists and forcibly removed her hands from the reins. A hot pain shot through Erin's bandaged hand and up into her arm. She bent over and breathed deeply, determined not to cry out.

"I'm real sorry," Tucker said. "I forgot about your hand. I sure didn't mean to hurt you none. Here, let me see."

Her hand did hurt, but not badly enough to let Tucker Gillam have his way. She would make him take her to the Kellers'. This was her chance.

"The blisters must have all broken," she said. "The bandage is soaked through. It might frostbite, mighten it, by the time we drive back to the house?"

"It would in this cold for sure," Tucker said. "Mattie usually has clean rags in her medicine bag to use for bandages. You might could wrap one over it to keep warm till we git home."

"Would you mind getting the bag? I don't think I feel up to crawling over the wagon seat."

"You set still, I'll fetch it."

Tucker put the reins down and stepped out of the sleigh so that he could reach into the back. Quickly, Erin picked up the lines and slapped them down hard on the horses' backs. The startled animals took off with a jerk, leaving poor Tucker in a snowdrift by the side of the road.

The homemade sleigh was harder to handle than Erin had anticipated. She tried to drive it straight, but it slipped to the right just as it started over the bridge, leaving one runner hanging precariously over the edge. Erin could hear the water rushing beneath the ice.

The horses balked and reared as the weight of the sled pulled them backward toward the river. There was a sickening sound of splintering wood as the team twisted in their harnesses and broke away from the sled. For a brief instant, the sled teetered on the edge of the bridge. Somewhere behind her, Erin heard Tucker call her name. Then the sled plunged down, breaking the ice and throwing her into the middle of the river.

Erin grabbed on to a log that lay partially submerged in the water and struggled to keep her head above the surface, but the weight of the sleigh pushed up against her with the full power of the river's current. "Dear God, help me!" she prayed. The sled shifted and sent her beneath the surface. She forced her head up, coughing and sputtering. She heard Tucker calling her, but she could not speak. The weight of the sleigh crushed against her chest. The sled pushed her under again, and she felt the frigid water go down her throat. Then everything went black.

ᴥ

The nothingness was quiet, warm, almost pleasant. But something was pressing on her back. Perhaps it was the sled. No, it was someone's hands, pushing. The hands let go, and Erin's lungs made an involuntary gasp for breath. The numbness disappeared, and she was caught up in a paroxysm of coughing that brought up quantities of water.

"Easy, Erin," the voice said. "Don't fight it, let it out. Now, try and breathe slow-like."

Tucker's hands pushed firmly on her back again. Erin struggled to sit up, but his hands were on her shoulders, forcing her to keep still. "Don't move around jist yet. Is there feeling in your arms and legs?"

Erin carefully moved each limb. "That's good," Tucker said. "Do you have especial bad pain anywhere?"

"My side hurts," she said hoarsely. "Where the sleigh had me pinned."

"All right now, roll over easy. Let me do all the work. Let's see can you sit up."

Tucker carefully lifted under her shoulders, and she managed to get in an upright position. She tried to focus her eyes, but it seemed as if she were looking through a red fog. She touched her hand to her forehead. There was blood on her fingers. Tucker already had his handkerchief out.

"Don't fret, Erin. The cuts ain't that bad. Head wounds always bleed like a stuck pig. It's nearly stopped."

Cold began to set in like Erin never could have imagined. It made the chill she'd felt earlier in the sleigh seem like a summer picnic. Her fingers and toes were numb and swollen, and her teeth chattered together so hard she was sure that they would break.

"We got to git you warm. There's nothing dry enough around here to build a quick fire. I reckon we'll have to walk on out."

Erin saw that Tucker's clothes were no dryer than hers and realized that he must have gone into the river after her.

"Tucker. . .I, I'm so sorry. Such a. . .foolish thing to do."

"Hush. Ain't no time for that."

"It will be dark soon, won't it?"

"We got no time to waste, that's a fact."

"The horses?"

"They're probably in the next county by now. Here, see if you can stand up."

Tucker lifted her to her feet. Immediately, her head began to swim. Her wool skirt hung in heavy, frozen folds; even her shoes were stiff.

"Can you put your arm 'round my neck?" Tucker asked.

Each step felt as if someone was sticking a knife into her ribs. They hobbled along for perhaps fifty feet until Erin's legs gave out. Tucker eased her down to the ground.

"I'm sorry," she gasped. "I can't do it. Leave me here and go get help, Tucker. I just want to go to sleep."

Tucker took a handful of snow and rubbed it roughly on Erin's cheeks.

"Stop!" she cried and tried to turn away.

"You can't go to sleep, you understand? You got to stay awake. We're going on." Tucker slipped his arm under Erin's legs and picked her up.

"You can't carry me all that way. . .it's too far."

"Never you mind. We'll make it."

The pain in Erin's side was no better with Tucker carrying her. Even though he tried to be careful, he couldn't avoid jolting and sliding in the snow. She could hear his heart pounding as he strained to get them back to the farmhouse.

The numbness was coming again, and Erin welcomed it. She wanted to be away from all the cold and pain. Through the mist in her mind she kept hearing Tucker's voice. He was trying to talk to her. He sounded so tired. Poor man. She wondered what he was saying. Then it was dark and warm, and she couldn't hear Tucker's voice anymore.

seventeen

Erin smelled coal oil. She opened her eyes and saw a lamp burning on the nightstand. Next to it sat the little brass clock. With so many quilts on her, how could she still be so cold? A violent shudder overtook her body, and she felt a horrible pain in her side. She looked at the sleeve of her flannel nightgown. At least she was dry. The wet wool skirt was gone.

Someone was coming in the room. "Tucker?"

Footsteps quickened across the floor. "You're awake. I heated up these flatirons and wrapped them in flannel. They'll help git you warm." He put the irons under the covers and sat down on the bed.

"Thank you." Erin touched the sleeve of his shirt. "You'd better change your clothes, too, or you'll be sick."

"Don't you fret about me. I worked up a good bit of sweat gitting us back here."

"I really am sorry. It was such a foolish, willful thing to do."

"Hush up." Tucker felt her cheek with the back of his hand. "Are you hurting?"

"Some. My side hurts when I breathe."

"Preacher's making a pot of tea. Think you can take some?"

"I'll try."

"How's your hand feel?"

Erin smiled weakly. "It's the only thing on me that's warm. It's infected, isn't it? That's why I have a fever."

"No, it's jist a little tender is all." Tucker did not meet her eyes. "I'll fix you up a bread and water poultice directly. It'll take the fire out. I sent Ben over to the Reynolds' place. Clay'll git the Doc here quick as he can."

Douglas came to the door with a cup in his hand, but when he saw Erin, he stopped. "Erin," he said. "My goodness. . ."

"Well, bring it on in," said Tucker. "She can't sip it from the doorway."

163

Douglas carried the cup to the foot of the bed, but he seemed reluctant to get any nearer. Erin's hair was matted with blood from the cuts on her forehead. She could feel scrapes and bruises all over her body.

"Give me that, Preacher."

Tucker's hand supported Erin's head while he held the cup to her lips. The warm tea tasted good, but after a few swallows, she was too tired to want any more. She turned her head away and closed her eyes.

Tucker's weight left the bed. Erin heard him put the cup on the nightstand and walk to the doorway. She could hear him and Douglas talking, but she was just too tired to keep her eyes open.

"Is she asleep?" Douglas asked.

"Maybe. It's hard to say with that fever. I wish the Doc would git here."

"Yes, so do I," said Douglas. "Tucker, this may not be the most appropriate time to ask, but you don't suppose there'll be any permanent disfigurement, do you? The hand is not so important, her sleeve could cover that, but what about the cuts on her face?"

"I'm not sure I understand your meanin', Preacher."

"You know, in my line of work. . .appearances can be important."

The conversation grew more intense, but they spoke quietly, and Erin could no longer make out what they were saying. She had the most peculiar feeling she had lost something that once had been very important to her, but it didn't seem to matter now.

There was a scuffling sound at the foot of the bed and then a crash. When Erin opened her eyes, she saw Douglas sprawled against the dresser. His lower lip was bleeding. Tucker stood in front of him with his fists doubled.

"I've seen some snakes in my time," Tucker said. "But you take the blue ribbon hands down. For two cents, I'd take you outside and fix your wagon."

"Tucker?"

Tucker turned away from Douglas and went to Erin.

"Lay back down," he said, pulling the quilt back across her chest. "You got to keep still until the Doc gits here and can bandage those ribs proper. I'm sorry, Erin. I won't hurt him no more. He jist made me so mad."

"It's all right, Tucker. I heard what he said." Erin looked wearily at Douglas.

"I thought you were asleep," said Douglas. "You misunderstood me. Certainly, my first concern is for your welfare."

"Your ring is in the box on the dresser," said Erin. "Please take it and go."

Douglas picked up the ring and turned it between his fingers. "Perhaps that would be best, for now," he said. "We'll talk when you are feeling better."

"Git out, Preacher," said Tucker.

"I didn't mean it like it sounded," said Douglas.

"Git out, now."

Douglas put the ring in his vest pocket and left without another word.

≈

Erin was vaguely aware of sounds and movements around her. At first, it was Tucker who seemed to be constantly fussing over her. His hands pressed a cloth on her forehead, and if she opened her eyes, he would try to make her drink. He kept putting something hot and wet on her hand. It made her hand hurt, but he put it on anyway. All Erin wanted to do was sleep. Why wouldn't he leave her alone?

After a while, there were other voices and other hands. Ben was there with ice cold spring water. He had such a frightened look in his eyes that Erin wanted to tell him not to be afraid, but she was too tired.

Then Jube came in, his loud voice filling the room, followed by a kind-looking man with gray hair. The man looked at Erin and tugged on his ear.

I must be really sick, Erin thought. *Lost Creek people only send for the doctor if you are very sick.*

Tucker and the doctor were talking. Erin thought they both looked sad. After a while, Dr. Stone sat down on the bed. "Can you understand me, Erin?"

Erin nodded her head.

"I'll be truthful with you," the doctor said. "That dunk in the river forced water into your lungs. You have the pneumonia. It ain't too bad yet, but it'll probably get worse before it gits better. The real problem is that infection from the burn on your hand. I don't know if your body can fight both things at once." Dr. Stone rubbed his chin thoughtfully. "Truth is, honey, if it gits much worse, I might need to amputate the hand to save your life."

Erin shook her head back and forth across her pillow. "No! I won't let you!" She pulled at the quilts, straining to get out of the bed.

"You lay back down, young lady," Dr. Stone said. "Those ribs aren't fully broken yet, but they will be if you start thrashing about."

Tucker reached across with a cool cloth to wipe the perspiration that beaded on her face. "Erin, listen to the Doc," he pleaded. "We're talkin' about your life."

Erin frantically searched for Tucker's hand. "You've got to promise me. Promise me you won't let him."

Tucker looked in agony. "I can't promise something like that, Erin."

"Please, Tucker. It's my choice. . .my life."

"Doc? Ain't there anything else you can do?" Tucker asked.

"Well," Dr. Stone said slowly. "We could try a drain. I've seen it work before, but it's chancy."

"Please, you've got to try it," Erin begged.

Dr. Stone thought for a moment. "All right, but I won't make any promises. Now, you settle back and rest."

Erin laid back, exhausted, and fell into a fitful sleep, but the smell of vinegar and mustard soon awakened her and made her cough. Dr. Stone was putting a vile-smelling poultice on her chest. Then came the smell of sulfa powder as the Doctor tended her hand. The hours passed by in a succession of evil-tasting medicines, compresses, and plasters.

There were softer hands on Erin's body now, changing her into a fresh nightgown. "Jist rest, child," Mattie said. "You're in the Lord's hands."

Erin tried to do as Mattie said, but one moment she was burning up and the next she was so very cold, and then it seemed as if her body was possessed by fits of coughing.

Everyone looked so concerned. Erin wanted to tell them not to worry, but it was too hard. It didn't matter anymore, she just wanted to sleep. She wanted to feel that warm numbness she had felt before.

Sleep finally came, and Erin gratefully began to slip further and further away. It seemed that all she needed to do was let herself go, and all the pain would be gone. If only something deep inside would allow her to give up so that she could find the rest her body craved.

∂

The heaviness was gone. There was no more burning heat in Erin's hand, and the weight had been lifted from her chest. She turned her head on the sweat-soaked pillow, and in the early morning light she saw Mattie sitting in a chair next to her bed. A Bible lay open in Mattie's lap, and her head rested on the chair back.

"Mattie?" Erin's voice had barely whispered, but the sound was enough to awaken one so accustomed to sleeping lightly by another's sickbed.

"Erin? Oh, Erin, praise God! I thought we'd lost you." Mattie's hand went instinctively to Erin's forehead. "Your fever must have broke during the night."

Erin lay still for a moment and tried to piece everything together. "You were at the Stiles' place, weren't you?" she asked. "Did Rose have her baby?"

"Rose had a strapping baby boy. I was beside myself with worry about you until I could find someone to tend Rose."

"How long has it been?" Erin asked.

"Four days since the accident."

"That long? The last I remember, Dr. Stone was here. He was talking to me about my hand." A terrible thought seized her, and she pulled her arm out from under the covers. She sighed with relief.

"The drains worked," said Mattie. "It was nip and tuck, but Doc's a good man."

"Are the Kellers all right?"

"Got their roof fixed and Becky's back is on the mend. Clay Reynolds went over and helped them after he got Doc for you."

"And Douglas, where is he? I don't remember seeing him since that first day."

Mattie didn't answer. Erin could tell by the look on her face that she was trying to decide what she should say.

"It's all right," said Erin. "Douglas is gone, isn't he?"

"Two days ago. Jube drove him out to Berryman. He figured to catch a ride to Steeleville and take the train from there. He said to tell you he 'regrets the situation.' I'm sorry."

"You were right, Mattie. You told me to seek the Kingdom first, but that's not what I did. I was more in love with the idea of having a family and a home of my own than I was with what God wanted to do in my life. Douglas and I are on two different paths."

"Don't fret about it, child. You know the saying, 'God never closes a door without He opens a window.'"

Winter sunlight streamed in the room. The snow glittered and sparkled in the yard. "It's so bright outside," Erin said.

"Does it bother you, child? I'll pull the curtain."

"No, don't. I think it's beautiful. It's good to see the light again. These past few days have been nothing but a dark blur."

"If you think you can handle it, I'll go warm you a cup of broth. I best wake Tucker on my way, and tell him you're back among the living."

"But it must be hours past sunrise," said Erin. "Why is Tucker asleep in the middle of the day?"

Mattie smiled. "You don't recollect anything, do you, child? Why, Tucker's been by your side day and night since the accident. Doc Stone finally came by last evening and threatened to beat him with an ax handle if he didn't get some sleep. He's been stretched out on the couch ever since. I'll go get him."

Erin could hear Mattie's voice, then Tucker's, and then the sound of heavy footsteps hurrying to her door. Tucker rushed into the bedroom, then stopped up short when he saw Erin. Tears welled up in the big man's eyes and ran down his cheeks. He moved the chair closer to Erin's bed and sat down. "You sure you're feelin' all right?" he asked softly.

"I'm not ready for another sleigh ride yet," said Erin. "But I'll be fine."

"Has Mattie told you everything that's happened?"

"She told me about Douglas. She also told me you've been wearing yourself out these past few days. I'm sorry I caused you so much worry."

"Erin, I've had a parcel of time to think whilst you was so sick. . .I've done considerable prayin', too. It come to me that I been mule stubborn with the Lord these last few years. Ain't no excuse for it. I knowed better. I jist turned away from His call. I'm so rock-brained it took almost losin' the most important thing in my life to git my attention."

"I'm not sure I understand."

"I reckon I am talkin' clear as mud." Tucker leaned over and took Erin's hand. "What I'm tryin' to say, Erin, is that I love you. I have since that first day you come bustin' in the barn door, but I jist wouldn't admit it. I know you're used to fancy courting, but the fact of the matter is that I'm rough as a cob about such things. I can't offer you much but a plain and simple life, but I give you my word, if you'd see fit to marry me, there'd always be a roof over our heads and food on the table. I'd do everything I could to make you happy." Tucker's eyes searched Erin's, waiting for a response.

Erin couldn't help thinking how different Tucker's proposal had been from Douglas'. There was no flattery, no promise of great status or wealth, just a pledge of love and loyalty.

She realized then she had found the real treasure. The home she had always craved could not be found with a handsome young man who had assurance of money and social position— but it was here with Tucker in a simple house where love was based on friendship and trust and their mutual faith in God.

"Tucker," she said. "I'd be proud to be your wife."

Tucker took her in his bearlike arms and held her close. When he touched her, she felt something deeper than she ever had with Douglas: a deep and abiding assurance that God had brought them together to this place, that He had a special plan for their lives, and that their love would continue to nurture and grow. The people of Lost Creek truly had become her people.

Erin was finally home.

A Letter To Our Readers

Dear Reader:

In order that we might better contribute to your reading enjoyment, we would appreciate your taking a few minutes to respond to the following questions. When completed, please return to the following:

Rebecca Germany, Editor
Heartsong Presents
P.O. Box 719
Uhrichsville, Ohio 44683

1. Did you enjoy reading *Lost Creek Mission*?
   ❑ Very much. I would like to see more books
       by this author!
   ❑ Moderately
       I would have enjoyed it more if _____

   _____

2. Are you a member of *Heartsong Presents*? Yes   No
   If no, where did you purchase this book? _____

   _____

3. What influenced your decision to purchase this
   book? (Check those that apply.)

   ❑ Cover   ❑ Back cover copy

   ❑ Title   ❑ Friends

   ❑ Publicity   ❑ Other _____

4. On a scale from 1 (poor) to 10 (superior), please rate the following elements.

___Heroine   ___Plot

___Hero   ___Inspirational theme

___Setting   ___Secondary characters

5. What settings would you like to see covered in *Heartsong Presents* books?

_____

_____

6. What are some inspirational themes you would like to see treated in future books?_____

_____

_____

7. Would you be interested in reading other *Heartsong Presents* titles?   ❏ Yes   ❏ No

8. Please check your age range:
❏ Under 18   ❏ 18-24   ❏ 25-34
❏ 35-45   ❏ 46-55   ❏ Over 55

9. How many hours per week do you read? _____

Name _____

Occupation _____

Address _____

City _____ State _____ Zip _____

Introducing New Authors!

__**Rae Simons**—*The Quiet Heart*—Thrilled at the opportunity to work near Liam, the love of her life, Dorrie has accepted a teaching position in a school for troubled children. Dorrie is desperate to please Liam and be the person he thinks she is. Will Dorrie ever possess a quiet heart? HP114 $2.95

__ **Birdie L. Etchison**—*The Heart Has Its Reasons*—Emily, the simple Quaker, wants only a simple life. But things get complicated when her dashing friend introduces her to handsome Ben Galloway. As she sorts through her conflicting emotions, Emily finds that love and committment are anything but simple decisions. HP123 $2.95

__**Mary LaPietra**—*His Name on Her Heart*—Marnette is haunted by her past. As God's plan unfolds, Marnette finds herself living with previously unknown relatives in the newly settled prairie. Although she constructs a tissue of lies about her past, Marnette is not as successful in denying her attraction to Drew Britton. HP124 $2.95

__**Elizabeth Murphey**—*Love's Tender Gift*—Determined to prove herself to Joel, Val decides to infiltrate a local cult as a class project. But she isn't prepared for her own vulnerability to the persuasive tactics of the cult. With Val's life in danger, Joel follows her to Ireland where she has been lured by promises of eternal life and love. Will Joel find Val in time to convince her that she already has his love...and God's? HP125 $2.95
